A MOON GIRL STOLE my FRIEND

WRITTEN and illustrated by
REBECCA PATTERSON

ANDERSEN PRESS

First published in 2019 by
Andersen Press Limited
20 Vauxhall Bridge Road
London SW1V 2SA
www.andersenpress.co.uk

2 4 6 8 10 9 7 5 3 1

British Library Cataloguing in Publication Data available.

ISBN 978 1 78344 798 5

This book is printed on FSC accredited paper
from reponsible sources.

Printed and bound in Great Britain by
Clays Limited, Elcograf S.p.A.

For the children at
Mayfield Primary School

CHAPTER ONE

Bianca had been planning her birthday since June. At a sleepover at mine in the summer holidays, we were floating about my room on the Float 'n' Sleeps and eating jellyfish crispies and I jumped from my Float 'n' Sleep onto hers and threatened to tip us both off if she didn't tell me every detail.

'You have to tell me! We're practically sisters!'

'Lyla! You're making me drop crispies everywhere!' She was giggling like mad and trying to keep her float steady. 'Stop it! We're crashing into the wall! I'm sliding off!' She was grabbing my leg now as I made her Float 'n' Sleep tip. 'Obviously I'll tell you! Just get back on your own float!'

I jumped back.

Bianca brushed crumbs off her knees. 'So . . . my granny said I can have the party at hers! You know she's got a pool. It's a pool party!'

'Oh! I love your granny!' I said. 'And I love her house!'

Bianca spun her Float 'n' Sleep around in the air with excitement. 'Also! Granny's going to make sure the concierge guy sets the weather to sunny and hot in the dome!'

Bianca's granny lives in the Havendome in the Outer Sector. It's a gated community. Quiet and super classy! I've been round a few times; Bianca's granny is an elegant old woman. Once she gave me and Bianca loads of her old perfume and we just poured it all over our heads and stank for weeks. No one would sit near us, but we didn't care – we called ourselves the Stink Sisters. That was when we were in Year Three.

Bianca lay down on her floating bed and looked up at my star-covered ceiling. 'But Granny said I really have to limit the numbers. Just invite my very best friends. She said the neighbours don't want to hear too many shrieking girls. Granny says it's six girls tops, so that's four friends plus you and me. But you know what some girls in our class are like if they're not invited to a party. We have to keep this party really, really quiet until I give out the actual invites.'

I had been so excited about the party I had bought Bianca's birthday presents early, just after we all went back to school in September. Really good presents! I got her a packet of Crazee stickers, the walking penguin ones.

You stick them on a wall and the second they're stuck they start walking about all over the place, like a cartoon. You never know where they'll get to. My mum doesn't let me have them as she doesn't want them wandering about and looking tacky on our walls.

I also got Bianca those flying sweets! The blackcurrant Jelly Gum Bats that you suck, and then open your mouth and they fly out! Mum doesn't let me have them either because they make a sticky mess on the ceiling. But I knew Bianca would be really pleased because we've been talking about getting some since the last sleepover at hers when we saw the advert.

I'd put the presents in the little hatch above my sleeping pod so I could admire them from my bed. They've been there almost three weeks now.

Gus stomped into my room. He's only six, little, so I don't know how he stomps so loud. He clambered right up onto my sleeping pod and said, 'Lyla! You didn't charge Sparks. He's not purring! He's just lying on the floor like he's DEAD!' Then he climbed over me as I lay there, walking up my back like I was a small mountain range.

'Get off, Gus! I'm asleep!'

'No. You're talking. It's Tuesday, school! Get up and fix Sparks! Why didn't you charge him?'

'I forgot,' I said, following Gus out of my room to find Sparks.

Sparks is our little cyborg cat. Sparks wakes up when you clap your hands and goes to sleep when you say: 'Bedtime, Sparks!' He's cute and small; he fits into your hand. But you have to let him charge up for about sixteen hours a day. It's my job to put him on his charging cushion at night so he's ready for the next day.

Gus used to fly Sparks around the kitchen in his Mars Mission toys. All Sparks's Mars Missions have been banned by Mum since Gus crashed Sparks into her omelette.

Another thing that Mum has banned is that aquagro cereal, Choccy Boom Blast – the kind where you put a drop of water onto a speck of cereal stuff and it swells up and fills the bowl with cereal and milk. Gus can't be trusted with it. He used to put way too much in his bowl, and then when he added the water he got a pile of cereal as big as him.

Anyway, we're always running late so we usually just grab a Vita-tab.

I chewed my Vita-tab and tried to get my stupid hair to stay flat. I always get this sprouty-up bit. I was squashing it down with gel when Mum yelled, 'Lyla, come on! Launch pad NOW! I have to be in Eastern Central Zone for a meeting at nine!'

I patted my hair as flat as I could, glanced at those perfect presents for Bianca, then ran up to the launch pad to join Mum and Gus in the skycar.

'Shove over, Gussy!' I said.

'Don't call me that, tufty head!'

'Well, shove up anyway!' I said, putting my hand over the sprouty bit of hair and keeping it there all the way to school to keep it flat.

Our skycar is so old it doesn't even have a transparent floor. That means we can't see directly below us, and one of the back jets is faulty too, so me and Gus always have to shove up together on the right side of the back seat to get it balanced when we fly. Mum hates doing a vertical takeoff; she always makes us check the airspace, saying, 'Is there anything above me? Look up, kids, anything coming over?'

'Nothing above me! All clear,' I said.

Mum fired up the jets and off we went, our skycar taking its place in the long line of traffic up in the Fly Zone.

'Bianca's having her party soon! She's giving out the invites today!' I said, looking out across the city and clouds. 'What should I wear? I wish my hair was long enough to do a bun!'

'It's a girls' party, Lyla, so it will be terrible,' said Gus. 'My best friend, Evan, he had Mr Dinosaur at his birthday and Mr Dinosaur makes a real, live, massive Triceratops from a bit of DNA! Right in front of you! He did it in Evan's front room but his mum wants a refund because the Triceratops did a bit of dinosaur wee on their carpet.

Bianca should definitely get Mr Dinosaur.'

Mum began bringing the skycar down onto the school launch pad. I could see Bianca below, already making her way to the Year Six portals.

'Right,' said Mum. 'We're here. Out, you two! See you later! Jump!'

Mum hates firing up the jets for takeoff, so she always makes us jump down while she hovers a little bit above the ground. We're used to it. Gus did his commando army roll when he landed and we both dashed down the launch-pad steps to the playground.

Gus ran off to the Infant Zone and I ran to catch up with Bianca. 'Hi! Did you give out the invitations yet?'

Bianca was shoving her coat into the suction hatch in the coatpod. 'Um . . . no . . . not yet,' she said, not quite looking at me. 'Lyla . . . I need to explain something. I've had to make the party a bit . . . different.' She just carried on squishing her coat into the hatch.

'Different? How?' I asked.

'Let me just hand out some invites and then I'll explain.'

Bianca opened her hand and there, right in the middle of her palm, was a print of a pink flower. It's the latest thing: instead of sending out the invitations electronically, the new craze is this – you get invites stored in your palm, and if you high-five a friend or shake their hand, the details of the party show up on their hand. It's supposed to 'promote a sense of closeness and wellbeing'.

'Ooh, Palmprintz! Having a party, Bianca?' said Mercedes, peering into Bianca's hand. 'I'm guessing the fabulous Mercedes Bonnay is on your hot party guest list?'

'You are!' said Bianca, giving her a high-five.

'And I take it you're inviting me too?' said Amia, doing her sassy little head flick.

'Sure,' said Bianca, shaking Amia's hand.

Mercedes looked into her palm. 'Wait! Does it wash off?'

'It fades,' said Bianca briskly, high-fiving Franka and Felicity.

Amia was gazing at her printed palm. 'I love the way the writing has come out glittery on our hands!'

'That's it! All done!' said Bianca, brushing hair off her face.

I held my palm out to her. 'Whoa, you forgot mine!'

She looked awkward. 'I didn't forget, Lyla, it's just . . . you know . . . I can't have just anybody this year.'

'How am I "just anybody"?!' I said. 'You've been talking to me about this party for weeks!'

'I know!' she said, walking towards the classroom portal. 'I thought you'd understand. I had to invite Mercedes and Amia, you know what they're like. Every girl in the class has been hassling me for an invite! I'm sorry, Lyla, I'll explain later.'

'What?' I said, but she was walking in front of me so I was talking to her back. 'Explain what?'

But she couldn't explain then as Mr Caldwell said, 'Less talking and more walking!'

Once we sat down in the class hub I said softly, 'So you invited four people, but you said you could invite five!'

Bianca looked ahead and mumbled, 'I'm sorry. I didn't want to upset you . . .' Then she turned round in her seat because someone was poking her in the back.

It was Petra Lumen!

Petra Lumen, whispering, 'Bianca, this will be my first Earth party!' and doing a tiny wave at Bianca, her palm all glittery with the invitation.

I looked at Bianca and hissed, 'You invited Petra instead of me?! She's only been here five minutes!'

'Three weeks and a day, actually,' muttered Bianca. 'She's new and I thought she might be lonely!'

Petra Lumen is NOT lonely! From the second she stepped into our class with her long, glossy Moon Colony hair she was invited to three sleepovers. Franka and Felicity have given her two tours around the Central Zone and the Trading Hub on two Saturdays in a row, and Amia has taken her to the Alpine Ski Sensadrome. James Defries is going to almost definitely ask her to the end-of-school disco too – even though that's not till June! He's been wearing the moonshades he got from his holiday last year every single day, even if it's rainy, just to look extra cool and impress her. She's always chatting to someone, swishing her hair about and laughing.

'Bianca, Petra is the opposite of lonely!' I said. 'She's the most popular person in our class since ever!'

'But that's not how she feels inside,' said Bianca.

I rolled my eyes.

Bianca looked at me hard, especially at my sprouty hair. 'OK, I wasn't going to even mention this, but Petra is surprised you and I are even friends. She said I was one of the few girls she could actually talk to here. But she said you seemed a little bit—'

'Enough talking, class!' said Mr Caldwell. 'Learning interfaces up, please!'

'What?' I whispered. 'A bit what?'

'Well . . . she said a lot of things about you,' muttered Bianca, looking straight ahead.

'When?'

'When I went to her house.'

'I didn't know you'd been to her house!'

'Well, why would you? We've not been close lately,' whispered Bianca, shrugging her shoulders a little.

'So I'm not invited, but she is?!' I said to the side of her face.

She turned her head and looked straight at me. 'Not everyone gets invited to every party, Lyla. We're not in Reception!'

Then Mr Caldwell said, 'Lyla! I've been watching you distract Bianca since you came in. Petra, could you swap places with Lyla? Thank you!'

As Petra and I pushed past each other between the desks Petra gave me a mean little jab with her elbow. And it wasn't a mistake.

CHAPTER TWO

Petra Lumen had arrived in the middle of a 'First Settlers of Mars' history lesson just over three weeks ago.

Miss Fritz, our really ancient cyborg receptionist and playground supervisor, brought her in. Miss Fritz is almost thirty years old and all her wires are starting to poke out. She has very slow word recall too, so when she came in with this new girl, Petra, she said, 'Hello, Mr Cald. Well. Here is the new. Stude.'

And loud boy Louis got told off for saying, 'A stude, Miss Fritz? Sounds like a vegetable!'

Miss Fritz blinked her big glassy eyes and carried on in her robotty voice, 'Stude . . . Stud. Ent. She is called . . . Petra Lu . . . men.'

'Thank you, Miss Fritz! Hello, Petra!' said Mr Caldwell, standing up to shake Petra's hand, like she was a grown-up. 'Class, let's give Petra Lumen our best Lime Grove Edu Hub welcome!'

So we all mumbled, 'Hello, Petra.' Felicity and Franka were so over-excited they waved madly to Petra from their desks.

Mr Caldwell grew up on the Moon and said it was wonderful to meet a fellow 'Moonite'. He said he hadn't been back to the Moon Colonies for years. 'It was all pretty grim and primitive back then,' he said, 'but I think it's all got a bit more exciting these days!'

'Oh, yeah! It is kind of flashy up there now!' said Petra in her smooth, Moon Colony accent. 'I've lived in Catena Yuri all my life; my mum's a mineral scientist and my dad's in ore export. We relocated to Earth for the schools.'

I don't know why anyone would relocate from the swanky Moon Colonies to send their child to Lime Grove Edu Hub with Mr Caldwell droning on about the history of Mars and Louis shouting out every five seconds, but Petra Lumen explained that her parents thought the Moon Colony schools were way too competitive.

Mr Caldwell said, 'Well, yes, we are a very friendly school!'

I remember Bianca whispered to me, 'She's so cool!' and she shoved our seats apart and asked Mr Caldwell if Petra could sit between us.

'Well, it's probably best if Petra takes that space behind you two,' he said. 'But how about you and Lyla show Petra around today – you can be her guides!'

And Bianca turned and smiled at me like we'd won a prize.

In the breaks that first day, Petra was surrounded by everyone, asking her how she got her hair so shiny and was it true everyone on the Moon lived in massive mansions? Even Louis, who never really talks to girls, was there, standing up on the little wall at the back and saying his uncle had worked in the Moon mines and did Petra know his uncle? She smiled at him and said, 'Well, no, the Moon is kind of . . . you know . . . big! I don't know everyone!' They all laughed like this was the best joke they'd ever heard.

At lunch we sat as a three with Petra between me and Bianca. It was mostly Petra and Bianca doing the talking. I just ate my noodles and caterfilla and listened to them discussing how they were both only children, and Petra was saying that probably made them way more outgoing and sociable than people with siblings. Bianca looked my way and said, 'Well, I'm mega sociable! But Lyla has a little brother. And I think you are a bit less outgoing than me, Lyla. You find it harder to make new friends, don't you?'

'Maybe,' I said, and walked off to spend a long time putting my rubbish into the degrader tubes.

Anyway, at the end of the not-getting-an-invitation-to-Bianca's-party day, Bianca came up to me in the coatpod. Petra was standing just behind us, putting on her silky Moon-girl coat thing.

Bianca came close to me and said, 'Lyla, we're still friends? Yeah?'

I pulled my coat out of my suction hatch and sighed, 'It's OK. It's your party. It's totally OK.'

But it *wasn't* totally OK. Bianca and I had been best friends for almost seven years. That's longer than my little brother has been alive!

'My dad's waiting on the launch pad!' said Petra. 'Come on, Bibi!'

Bibi! When was Bianca ever called Bibi?! Never! And I should know because I met Bianca on day one, in Nursery, and we were best friends. We just got on straight away, and we said we were the Magic Princess Twins because our hair was the same length then.

One of the best things about Bianca is that she can add really good stuff to any game. In Year One she made up this game called 'Get the Bogwitch!'

It was a really dark, windy winter playtime and we were playing a game with twigs by the real bushes and the perimeter fence. I can't remember what we were doing with the twigs, but the wind dropped for a moment, the leaves stopped rustling and we heard a voice saying something like, 'Shadow!' on the other side of the fence! We were so scared! It was brilliant. We both heard it.

It wasn't like one of us pretended to hear it and the other person went, 'Oh yes, me too!' We *both* did.

'It's . . . THE BOGWITCH! Get the power twigs!' said Bianca.

Every playtime after that, Bianca and I would be over there by that bit of the perimeter fence making all sorts of stuff up about the Bogwitch on the other side. Bashing power twigs on the fence and yelling, 'Bogwitch! We can smell you!'

Soon loads of people wanted to join in. And there would be masses of us whacking our power twigs on

the fence. Eventually we had to make a rota to say who could play when. We were spending more of the play time sorting out the rota than actually playing. James Defries got really cross when he wasn't on the rota and shouted at everybody, 'Idiots! No one lives over there – it's just old broken houses!'

Bianca said very slowly, 'James, you didn't HEAR what we HEARD!' And then she and I held our twigs above our heads and said, 'THE BOGWITCH said SHAAAADOW!' That's all it took to send everyone off running around the playground with the power twigs and screaming 'BOGWITCH!' all over again.

Bianca made little maps and messages from the Bogwitch at home, and she'd bring them to school and show everyone and say stuff like, 'This here on the map is the deadly death pit! Right by this huge statue of a griffin is the Tower of the Mighty Bogwitch with all these skulls round the top!'

And we didn't really believe her, but at the same time we did.

Eventually it got out of control with masses of kids playing it, but not playing it properly, just yelling and bashing big sticks on the perimeter fence. The head teacher, Mrs Fradley, did this big assembly about the dangers of playing with twigs and said if she ever caught somebody so much as touching the perimeter fence, never mind hitting it, there would be serious consequences and did she make herself quite clear! It's funny, you hear the little kids talking about the

Bogwitch now like it's a fact, when it was just me and Bianca making stuff up.

Even now we're older, if we're having a sleepover and it's really late, Bianca does her old Bogwitch voice in the dark, whispering 'Shaaaadow!' And I always end up hiding under the covers going, 'Stop talking about it! You are freaking me out!'

When we were in Year Two we both got married to James Defries. We weren't in love with him and he wasn't being cool then in his moonshades and would still play weddings. We all just wanted a massive wedding in the lunch-time break.  Felicity was the vicar because her mum is an actual real-life vicar and she knew all the words for getting married. She married us in a ceremony by the flyke sheds. She found some little caterpillars in a real bush and made us put them on our noses.

Bianca said that wasn't what happened in a real wedding but Felicity said, 'I think I should know HOW to marry someone! My mum's in charge at St Giles Omni Faith!'

After the caterpillars on the noses bit we all ran out into the playground and the whole class joined in, chasing after us and singing, 'HERE COME THE BRIDES!' Miss Fritz got all overheated shuffling after everybody, trying to calm us down. Bianca, James, Felicity and I got lined up in a corridor by Miss Fritz doing her electro-command voice and then we got really told off by Mrs Fradley for messing about by the flyke sheds and we had to miss the afternoon break.

But even now I only have to say, 'With this caterpillar I thee wed,' and Bianca and I start laughing. Sometimes I whisper it in a quite serious assembly about anti-bullying or the First Moon Mineral War, and we just have to have the silent, shaking, cannot-stop-giggles.

Before Moon Girl arrived we had a sleepover at each other's houses nearly every week. We know each other's houses so well it doesn't feel like a sleepover. Our mums just leave us alone to get on with stuff. Which is probably why, when we were six, we broke her family teleporter.

We tried to teleport all her teddies to my house. But it was the kind of teleporter that's only supposed to send food – an old model. We shoved all her teddies into the sending hatch and pressed the buttons, but the teddies just disintegrated and messed up the whole machine.

Bianca's dad went totally mad when he saw the melted fur all over the inside of the teleporter. He really yelled at Bianca, but not so much at me, as I was just the visiting child. He was shouting, 'Do you have ANY IDEA how much a teleporter costs to replace, young lady?'

The really good thing was, though, that one teddy did successfully teleport to my house!

Except he'd arrived really, really small, shrunken by the teleportation process. Like this! Bianca said I could keep him, and I still have him. I keep him up on that hatch above my sleeping pod, the one where I put Bianca's birthday presents.

I call him Nano Ted.

Bianca can do amazing accents, and every time Bianca and I meet we do a really stupid but hilarious (to us) greeting we have perfected since the end of Year Five. We pretend we're teenagers from the Moon Colonies and put on our Moon Colony accents and say, 'Today ain't no Moon day and this Earth day is too long for me!' and we do the handshake thing you see them do in all the shows.

We do it all the time. Well, we used to, but on the Monday before Bianca handed out her invitations, Petra caught us playing it in the coatpod and said in her real Moon Colony accent, 'To be honest, you two sound more Canadian than Moonite!'

Bianca said, 'Oh no! Do we?! That's soooo funny! It's just a silly game Lyla makes me play! You're not upset, are you?'

'Not at all,' said Petra, smiling and looking sort of shy. 'People always try to copy me. I'm kind of used to it!'

So I said, 'We weren't copying you. We played it before you arrived.'

'*We played it before you arrived.*' Petra mimicked my voice to make it sound really babyish. 'I bet you did, like your Bogwitch game – I've heard all about that too. Get some new friends, Lyla . . . maybe your brother's age?'

Bianca didn't say anything. She just bit her lip.

CHAPTER THREE

So that's how it happened, just four weeks into a new term and I wasn't invited to my best friend's birthday. It was Friday evening and I was stroking Sparks, lying in my sleeping pod and thinking about all this instead of doing my homework. Gus came into my room with purple stuff all round his mouth.

'What's that?' I said, pointing at it.

'Nothing, can I have a go with Sparks now?'

'What did you eat?'

'I can't remember. Nothing,' he said, looking straight at me. And as he stood there with his purple face I saw a tiny sticker of a penguin walk out of the neck of his top and make its way towards his ear.

Then I looked up to the hatch above my sleeping pod. The presents for Bianca had . . . GONE!

I jumped up and lifted his top to reveal his babyish six-year-old tummy covered with Crazee stickers. The ones I'd bought for Bianca!

The penguins were marching about all over his tummy. 'They tickle,' he said, 'but I know Mum doesn't like them walking on the walls.'

'BUT THEY'RE NOT FOR YOU! THEY'RE FOR BIANCA'S BIRTHDAY NEXT WEEKEND!'

'I forgot,' he said.

Then I saw he had the screwed-up wrapper of the Jelly Gum Bats in his hand. 'YOU ATE ALL THE SWEETS TOO!'

'Lyla, remember, indoor voice, please!' he said.

And then I started crying. Not because of the sweets and the stickers, but the whole 'not being invited to my only best friend's birthday' thing and for not being 'mega sociable'. And my tears and snot were dripping onto Sparks.

Gus patted my head and said, 'You're snotting on Sparks. Sorry. It was an accident I ate them and used all the stickers.'

'I know,' I sighed. 'Sorry I shouted so loud in your face.'

'We can get her another present tomorrow!' he said.

'Oh . . . it doesn't even matter because I'm not actually invited to her birthday party now,' I said, trying to wipe the teary snot off Sparks.

'Why? Did you do something bad? Did you bite Bianca?'

'No, people don't bite each other in Year Six. They just talk about hair all day.'

'Boooring!' said Gus, turning to go. 'You can keep Sparks a bit longer because you're sad.' And he shuffled out of the room, a penguin sticker now making its way up into his hair.

Like I said, usually Bianca comes to my house at the weekend or I go to hers, but not this weekend. Not last weekend, either, though I didn't know why then. I moped about all Saturday morning. Gus and I played a bit of Moon Wars with his action set. I tinted Sparks's fur pink. I got the pink all over the floor in the hall.

I got in trouble with Mum.

And later, Dad got even crosser with Gus when the food delivery arrived.

'Gus, can you explain why we need thirty-five bars of chocolate?!'

Gus was just standing by the new food delivery, looking down at his socks. 'Um . . . Because we like it?'

Dad was unpacking more stuff. 'Where's all the veg?! What are these?'

Gus looked up. 'Those are cake buttons! Just add

water to one tiny button thing and it grows into an absolutely massive chocolate cake! "Convenient for the busy restaurant owner!" Says so, on the advert!'

'I'm not running a restaurant!' said Dad. 'I was planning on making my caterfilla risotto tonight! And now, thanks to you, we'll be eating cake buttons!'

'Oh good! Risotto is icky,' said Gus, but Dad gave him an I-am-NOT-a-happy-dad look.

Dad went back to shoving packets of stuff away into cupboards and muttering to himself, 'You would think that by NOW they would have invented a self-ordering fridge that has the common sense not to take orders from a SIX-year-old!'

'I can trick it!' said Gus. 'I open the door and put on my deep voice and it thinks I'm you. Watch!'

He opened the fridge door and the fridge said, 'Hello. State your order,' in its polite lady fridge voice.

Gus put on a deep Dad voice and said very quickly, 'Five micro boxes of Choccy Boom Blast cereal, three packets of blackcurrant flying Jelly Gum Bats! Oh . . . and . . . do they do stickers? Maybe? A packet of Crazee stickers . . .'

Dad slammed the fridge door shut. 'That's enough, Gus!'

'Delivered by teleportation today, Mr Hastings?' said our fridge from inside its closed door.

'Yes!' said Gus to the fridge in his deep Dad voice before running out of the kitchen.

'The little . . .' said Dad through gritted teeth. 'Well, we can't wait for another delivery now. Teleporting's so slow on Saturdays. We'll have to do this old-school style and actually go OUT to buy food!'

He flew us to the Trading Hub. Just at the side of the main hub, there's a strange vintage market where you can buy real, fresh food from real people behind these stalls.

Mum won't go anywhere near it because she says it's unhygienic.

As we came down to land on the Trading Hub, Gus was doing his thing of counting stuff he could see in the air. 'Two skybuses, three Volkswagen Auto Airs, and ooh, there's the Central Zone London Metropolis shuttle! Some people on flykes . . . Hey! Lyla, look out my side, it's your friends!'

I saw them, just below us in the Flyke Zone – Bianca and Petra, both on their flykes, pedalling like crazy and laughing. Bianca was doing her aerial loop-the-loop.

'There's Bianca!' said Gus. 'With Moon Girl! See them, Lyla? Wave!'

'They should be a bit more careful on flykes, especially at this altitude!' said Dad.

We passed them and I didn't wave. I ducked right down so they couldn't see me. 'You didn't wave!' said Gus. 'Oh. I remember. Bianca didn't invite you to her party. You don't like her any more.'

'Shh!' I said.

'What's this?' said Dad. 'Since when?'

So I had to explain to Dad, and then he told Mum about it later while he was stirring his risotto! And then Mum looked at me all concerned and said, 'Lyla, love, there must be some mistake! I'm sure Bianca didn't mean to upset you. We can sort it!'

I said, 'It doesn't need sorting! It really doesn't!'

But then she called Bianca's MUM! She flipped out her Chatcom, got it on hologram and there, floating in our kitchen, was a hologram of Bianca's mum. Usually Mum has it set to normal so the other people's heads are the same size as yours while you chat, but Gus always messes with our Chatcom, so Bianca's mum came up into the room massive. Filling the whole room!

Gus explained, 'I put it onto Stadium format. Her nostrils look like massive tunnels!'

Mum put her finger up to her lips and glared at Gus while she started talking to Bianca's mum. I couldn't bear to listen to the conversation so I ran off and hid my head under the sofa cushions to block out the total cringe.

Gus came in a few minutes later and poked my leg. 'You can come out now. You're going to the party, and at the end of the call I waved to Bianca and Moon Girl in the background! I blew them a kiss!'

'What? Petra and Bianca saw Mum's call?!'

'Yes, they're having a nice sleepover,' said Gus cheerily.

CHAPTER FOUR

On Monday, when I arrived at school, Bianca just sat on the low wall by the classroom and watched me walk towards her. She didn't wave. When I got there she gave me a tight little smile and said, 'It's not cheap having these Palmprintz invites done, you know? Hold out your hand.'

I held out the palm of my hand. Bianca opened hers and there was a new party invitation imprint. No high-five. She just mushed her palm down onto mine. 'There,' she said. 'Now, where's Petra? She's late.'

I looked at the party invitation printed on my palm and said, 'Look, I know my mum phoned your mum on Saturday . . . but . . . I didn't tell her to, she just did.'

'Whatever,' said Bianca, looking straight out across the playground, then she jumped up saying, 'Whew! She's here!' and started waving to Petra.

Petra walked up to us. 'Hi, Bianca! Brilliant sleepover! Your house is adorable!' Then she turned to me and said, 'You know, Lyla, up on the Moon Colonies we don't get our mummies to sort out our social lives.' She and Bianca huddled together on the wall. Petra said, 'So, I see you two didn't come in costume today? I didn't. I'm not spending the whole day looking like a weirdo.'

It was only then I remembered that it was the day of the Year Six history trip to the 'Yesterday Village' in a place called Peterborough Sector Five. I'd been so busy being miserable all weekend about Bianca I'd forgotten all about it.

You're meant to dress up like people from the olden days for the trip. My mum says she's got better things to do than make 'jeans' by drawing fake stitches onto a perfectly good pair of Pristalyne school trousers.

Felicity turned up with a bit of wire over her teeth. 'What's that supposed to be?' said Bianca.

'A brace. It's how they used to straighten wonky teeth before they could do it all with genetics.' Felicity did a wide grin to show the wire. 'See!'

'Looks dumb!' said Petra.

Then James turned up with an old bit of cardboard with a picture of an apple he'd drawn on the back. 'Authentic recreation of an iPad!' he said, did some pretend swiping and said in an old grandad voice, 'Now, just let me check on the weather and me old selfies!'

Petra threw back her head laughing, and said, 'James! You're the funniest!' He went bright red.

As usual, Mercedes turned up on her persojet, flying high above the playground and leaving a blue smoke trail that read:

YEAR SIX TRIP TODAY! ... MERCEDES RULES THE SKY!!!!!

Mercedes comes to school on her persojet every day. She's the only one in our school with one. She flies it all around the playground (not allowed) every morning and sets the jets to coloured smoke so she leaves a trail everywhere (totally not allowed).

She landed up on the launch pad and took off her helmet. 'Check out my feet, guys!' she shouted down to us. 'Look, from my grandma! Do you know what they are?' She had some funny-looking shoes on with stringy stuff to do them up. She was waggling her feet as she clomped all the way down the launch-pad steps looking really pleased with herself. 'I'll tell you what they are! Only genuine twenty-first century . . . *trainers*!'

Mr Caldwell came out to tell her off

about the persojet and let
us into the class hub.

Mr Caldwell takes the
trip to Yesterday Village
really seriously. Every year
he dresses up completely like
an olden times person. He makes
his teeth look bad and wears these glasses things they
all used to wear. He's even got a vintage jumper with
those real actual button things on that work to fasten it
together, and he has a bag with a real zip.

Everybody always wants to play with the zip.

I didn't have to look to know that Petra and Bianca
would be partners on the skybus.

And for the first time ever I was the spare person.
Mr Caldwell said, 'No partner for the skybus, Lyla?
How about you team up with Miss Fritz?'

Miss Fritz waved her funny fake-
looking hand at me and said, 'We
can. Be. Friends. What . . . fun.'

Louis muttered, 'Good luck
with old battery head!'

Luckily Mr Caldwell didn't hear — he gives out detentions if he hears any robotism.

I could've sat with Louis, but Mr Caldwell said what he always says when we go on school trips. 'Louis, you'd better be with me.'

'Why?' said Louis.

'I think we know why,' said Mr Caldwell.

We all know why. Louis tried to burn a packet of jellyfish crispies with a magnifying glass on a skybus when we were on a school trip to the Tidal Energy Centre in Year Three.

'That was ages ago!' said Louis. 'Nothing even went on fire!'

The only good thing about being tragically partnered with Miss Fritz is that you get to sit right at the very front of the skybus where the floor is see-through. I could see all of the Eastern Central Zone below, and all the skycars flying underneath on the flyway really fast.

When we took off I looked down at the playground and tried to work out where we'd thought the Bogwitch lived all those years ago in Year One.

Just to make a bit of conversation I said, 'No one lives in those old houses any more, do they, Miss Fritz? Those ones by the fence?'

She tilted her head on one side and said, 'Will commence aerial scan.'

'Oh, you don't have to! I was only wondering,' I said.

But after a bit or electrical humming and buzzing she said, 'The area is eight thousand and forty-two square metres. Contains twelve dwellings dating from the nineteenth century. Classified uninhabitable. Many life forms present. Over eight hundred million insect forms. Four hundred and eleven bird forms. Nine hundred reptiles and two hundred and ninety-seven mammals.'

'Thanks!' I smiled at her, and as I didn't really want any more cyborg chat I just looked out of the window. If you look out of the left side of the skybus you can see the thin silver line of sea in the distance and everyone always shouts, 'I can see the SEA!'

Then Mr Caldwell always stands up and says, 'Thank you, Year Six! I think we've all established this fact!'

· *·⭐.* ·

The good, quiet kids were all in the middle part of the skybus playing on their holograms and taking their flying sickness tablets like old ladies.

Louis was sitting next to Mr Caldwell, saying, 'Do you remember iPads, sir, from when you were little?'

Mr Caldwell was laughing and saying, 'Well, Louis, I know I look old but I'm not *that* old!'

Right at the back of the skybus Mercedes had got all the other girls singing. She was leading them in the usual skybus school trip songs like, 'We're a Mile in the Air But We Don't Care'.

Then I heard Petra say, 'Wait, I know loads of really, really cool Moon Colony songs!' And she started everyone singing a song that is a bit parental guidance explicit. Petra was standing up facing backwards, which is probably illegal, conducting. Loads of girls were also standing up in their seats and doing inappropriate moves, while Bianca and Franka were doing the drum beats with their hands on the backs of the seats.

Miss Fritz made her slow, robotic way to the back of the skybus, pulling her version of an angry face, and said, 'I. Really expected. More. From you. Young ladies!'

Mr Caldwell said, 'Miss Fritz, would you mind sitting with them at the back to supervise? I thought this was a Year Six class but apparently it's Reception and they can't be trusted to sit still and be quiet!'

Petra and Bianca and Mercedes all had to sit at the front with Mr Caldwell, and this meant I was put next to Louis. I said, 'Hi, Louis,' but he just sighed and didn't say anything to me the whole way to Yesterday Village.

Everyone clapped when we landed. They always do.

Once we'd all got off the skybus, Mr Caldwell got very excited, saying, 'This, children, is an old CAR PARK! Look at the white lines! Painted by hand by people many years ago to show where every land car could park!'

'Boring snoring,' muttered Louis.

We were put into groups. Bianca and Petra were both with Mr Caldwell's group. Mr Caldwell was being all old-fashioned and putting on his old-time voice and saying, 'LOL! Just look at my buttons and look at my glasses. I'm Short-Sighted!' And Bianca and Petra were laughing and joining in, saying, 'Oh! OMG! Amazeballs, your TRAINERS are to die for!' And their whole group was falling about laughing as they walked off into the 'How We Used to Holiday' section.

This was the first school trip I hadn't been in the same group as Bianca, but she didn't even look back at me as her group walked away.

CHAPTER FIVE

Yesterday Village has a real old house that they have filled with all the old junk from ages ago. It's a bit boring. The worst part about it is they have all these attendants dressed up as old-fashioned people talking in silly olden days voices. In the 'At Home – Living Without Robots' section, you walk into the hall and this man greets you in an old-fashioned suit and he says, 'Hello! Kids, welcome to my house! The year is 2020 and this, my little friends, is my TIE! The TIE was worn by men going out to work. It was for decorative purposes only. Now, come this way and you can see how we used to cook!'

Miss Fritz had to poke Louis because he was groaning and muttering, 'Like I care,' to himself. Then we all had to shuffle about an old-style kitchen and Miss Fritz said we had to draw something called a Dish Washer.

Then we went upstairs and we met this other attendant person and she also talked to us like we were all about five and said, 'Gosh, MODERN children! Don't you look healthy! Look at your beautiful clothes! I'm wearing a SKIRT. It's made from WOOL. From a sheep!!'

Everyone went, 'Ugh! Gross!' and she carried on, 'Well, if you want to see something really nasty, then step this way!' She opened a door and, raising one eyebrow, said, 'Girls and boys! I present THE TOILET! Or THE LOO, as one might have called it!'

There was an old-fashioned toilet. She said people used to wipe their bottoms with this paper on a roll.

'What, using their BARE hands?!' said Mercedes.

'Yes!' she said. 'But then they washed them here with the soap in this basin.'

Then she said the poo wasn't vaporised and converted into useful methane gas like we do now. It was flushed away into sewers in just water.

Miss Fritz had to tell everyone, 'Stop being . . . VERY silly!' because Amia, Louis and Mercedes were making I'm-going-to-be-sick noises.

Then the woman said, 'We are very lucky at Yesterday Village because this TOILET actually works! Who would like to try and flush it?'

At this point, Louis and Amia and Mercedes and the rest of our group started backing out of the room into the corridor going, 'Oh, gross . . . oh, gross . . . no way!' And while Miss Fritz trundled out with them to give them a talking-to about how she expected Year Six to behave with more maturity, I was left alone with the attendant to try the flushing of the loo.

There was a poo in there, but the attendant said that for obvious health and safety reasons this was just a model poo. I flushed it. The poo went. It was easy. The woman in the sheep skirt said, 'Very brave! Imagine having to do that every day!'

We all sat outside for lunch and they gave us real old-style food they make in the museum. We got something called a hot dog. Louis said, 'Miss Fritz? What kind of dog was a hot dog? What part of the actual hot dog are we eating here?!'

Miss Fritz was looking a bit hot herself; a little puff of steam was rising from her head. I suppose she's usually just sitting about not doing much on a normal school day, so this was quite exhausting for her. She just turned her head to Louis and said slowly, 'Probable answer: sausage dog, now extinct.'

'Fair enough,' said Louis. 'Tastes OK, though!'

They made us try something called cola, but we could only have a tiny sip. I liked it and Louis took big gulps saying, 'Wow, they should bring this stuff back!'

Bianca and Petra didn't touch it, and James Defries said, 'I'll pass thanks! I try not to drink anything that contravenes the International Poison Act. My dad's a doctor.'

While we were all finishing our weird lunches I went over to Petra and Bianca's table. 'Hi, so did you do the toilet bit yet?' I asked.

Bianca hardly looked up at me. 'Um . . . no . . . Don't think we did, did we, Petra?'

'No, not yet, we just saw the rooms where they all worked called offices, with old equipment and wires everywhere,' said Petra, still looking down at her hot dog thing.

'I was the only person who would flush it!' I said.

'Great,' said Petra in a bored voice, then she got up and said, 'Come on, Bibi! I think we've got better things to do than talk about flushing toilets. I can't eat any more of this disgusting old stuff. Let's find the degraders!'

And they went. Walking arm in arm, singing that Moon Colony song they were singing on the coach and carrying their unwanted food.

They didn't say bye.

At the end of the afternoon we all had to go round the Transport bit together. We had to sit and watch a really old film of all the traffic on the roads and see poor old-fashioned children just stuck inside gloomy houses with their really rubbish computery things.

An attendant was dressed up in a funny bright-yellow jacket. He put on a dramatic sad face and said, 'In the olden days all the cars were on . . . the ground! Right by children's houses. Just imagine those poor little children, always getting run down by the cars and living right by the dirty roads. If they ventured out without proper care and attention, many children just rolled into the busy roads and . . . died a tragic death! Those that didn't perish suffered a lifetime of breathing problems and untold misery!' He bowed his head for dramatic effect.

Mr Caldwell looked like he was about to cry! 'Those poor children! It's hard to imagine, isn't it, Year Six? Think just how much better our lives are now!'

'Mine would be even better if I wasn't stuck in this stinky old museum,' said Louis.

I think Miss Fritz wanted to say, 'Less of the cheek, Louis,' but as she was low on power it just came out as, 'Less . . . cheese.'

Louis thought this was so funny he asked Miss Fritz more questions as we all made our way back to the skybus. 'Miss Fritz! What's her name?' he said, pointing to me.

Miss Fritz turned her slow eyes towards me and said, 'LOW BATTERY ALERT.'

'Ha! Ha! Hear that, Lyla? Miss Fritz thinks you're called Low Battery Alert!'

'Shh! Louis, you're wearing her out!'

'No, she's fine. Hey, Miss Fritz! Here's a tough one, can you do thirty-four times ninety-two in your head?'

Miss Fritz turned very slowly to look at Louis, but then froze and stopped moving altogether. 'Now you've done it!' I said. 'She's lost power!'

'MR CALDWELL! OLD FRITZY'S CRASHED!' yelled Louis.

Mr Caldwell was furious. 'Why is that, Louis?! Anything to do with you? And Lyla, I'm disappointed in you!'

'But, Mr Caldwell . . . I . . . we didn't mean to . . . she just crashed,' I stammered.

'Well, I think both of you can be responsible for getting poor Miss Fritz back to the bus where she can be plugged into a charging point before we take off and fly back to school. Neither of you will be visiting the museum gift shop! And it would be a kindness to Miss Fritz if you both stayed in one break time and polished all the maths learning helmets for her.'

Louis and I began lifting Miss Fritz slowly back to the bus. 'You're so stupid,' I muttered to Louis.

'Not my fault! If this school bothered to get us better cyborg staff this wouldn't happen. Her battery brain is ancient!' he said, wheezing as he carried Miss Fritz's robot legs.

All the class walked past us laughing, and Petra and Bianca overtook us swinging these cute little bags full of souvenirs from the museum gift shop. I heard Petra whispering to Bianca, 'Breaking robots for fun, so immature!'

'But I think it was an accident, wasn't it?' said Bianca.

I nodded at her and rolled my eyes towards Louis.

· ✶·⭐.✶ ·

Back on the coach, we had to sit in exactly the same places, so I was next to Louis.

Miss Fritz, now fully recharged, went up and down doing the head count, 'Alert. Missing one! WHO?'

'Um, it's Amia, miss!' said Mercedes. 'Still in the souvenir shop! Getting stuff to take to Bianca's party!'

We saw Amia coming, carrying bags of stuff from the souvenir shop. She was trying to run but the big bags were slowing her down. She got onto the skybus, puffing. 'Don't know how they managed in the old days carrying all this shopping about, Mr Caldwell! My arms are falling off!'

'Well, yes, hurry up and sit down,' said Mr Caldwell. 'What have you bought? Looks like you cleared out the whole shop.'

Amia started making her way to her seat, crashing the bags into people's legs as she walked down the aisle. 'Sorry, Mr Caldwell . . . I couldn't resist. It's all for Bianca's pool party on Sunday: vintage lip gloss and tons of really weird sweets . . . Look – something called chewing gum!'

She had now plonked herself down in her seat.

All the way back to school all the girls were discussing Bianca's party. Loudly.

'So, girls, I'm going to be wearing a Luna silk top!' said Petra. 'Or . . . no . . . maybe, my rose-gold shimmer skirt . . . or my top with the goldfish print that looks like a moving aquarium . . . Or . . . Oh! I don't know! I just CAN'T make up my mind!'

And all the girls laughed and Franka said, 'You'd look good in anything!'

And Petra put her head on one side and said, 'Well, I was a model.'

'No way!' said Mercedes.

'I can see why,' said Bianca.

'Well, it was a long time ago,' smiled Petra. 'I was only a few months old! A baby! It's sooo embarrassing! I'm that baby on the packets of Vaporiser Poo Poo Go Nappypants!'

'I've seen them! I walked past a whole stack of them in the Trading Hub!' said Felicity.

'Yes,' said Petra. 'I'm still on them, my baby face!'

'But you could be a model now!' said Bianca.

'Well . . . maybe,' said Petra.

'Definitely!' said Bianca.

Louis said to me quietly, 'You can see why I don't talk to girls!'

'*I* am a girl,' I said, but I didn't say anything else all the way back to school. I looked out at the clouds and the sun setting behind. If you look really far out, you can see those huge London Skyport towers on the horizon, and the old pointy Shard building between.

On the way home in the skycar Gus was really shocked when I told him I'd been round Yesterday Village with Louis. He said, 'Are you crazy? LOUIS? He set fire to a skybus! It crashed to earth as a giant fireball, BOOM! Evan told me!'

'He didn't set fire to a skybus! He tried to set fire to a jellyfish crispies packet. And it was ages ago!' I said, getting out of the skycar and onto our launch pad.

'Ooh, what's that glitter in your hand!' said Gus.

I looked at the Palmprint for Bianca's party. 'Bianca's invitation,' I said. 'But I don't have a present for her now . . . thanks to you!'

We went into the hall. I clapped Sparks awake and picked him up for a little cuddle as I walked down to the kitchen.

Gus trotted behind. 'No! But thanks to ME you DO have a present! I ordered all the extra stuff through the fridge on Saturday when Dad got cross! Remember? It all came! I ordered more flying Jelly Gum Bats and more stickers – look! Mum put them here.' He patted a pile of packets on the shelf proudly.

I picked up the replacement presents. 'Good! But what will I *wear*?'

'Clothes,' said Gus, lifting Sparks out of my arms. 'Don't make him pink again, Lyla, he hates it.'

CHAPTER SIX

In the end I decided to wear my colour-change top; it changes colour when you move a lot. It's quite old now but I like the big bow on the shoulder. Mum flew me to the party in the Havendome and Gus came too, so he could see what the Havendome is like.

He was excited. 'Is it for zillionaires?'

'Not really, Gus,' said Mum, doing one of her dangerous undertaking moves where she flies the skycar under a slower skycar and then zooms up in front. She looked back at me and smiled. 'Happy, Lyla?'

'I would be if I thought Bianca even wanted me there!' I said moodily.

'Course she does!' said Mum. 'She invited you.'

'Only because you made her!' I snapped back.

Mum muttered, 'Ten going on fourteen! Really, Lyla, stop being so silly. You've been nothing but sulks these last few days. Whatever little argument you and Bianca had is over and I bet you have a wonderful time today!'

The Havendome is a lot of big houses under a huge glassy dome. You have to fly the skycar to the security robot who's in a spherical, see-through office right on the top of the dome, and then it gives you clearance to enter, the top hatch opens and you fly down inside.

'It's like a beautiful dream!' said Gus. 'LOOK! They have parrots! They have palm trees down there! Swimming pools! Let's live here!'

'No thanks,' said Mum. 'It's a lot of old people playing golf.'

'I can learn golf,' said Gus.

Inside the dome the weather was sunny. Our skycar flew down between little fluffy clouds to Bianca's granny's roof.

'As Lyla is nothing-but-sulks, maybe I should go instead?' said Gus, undoing his seatbelt.

'No, Gussy!' said Mum.

I jumped down from the skycar and said, 'It's a GIRLS' party, Gus, remember. They're "terrible"! Bye!'

Bianca's granny's house is huge. It's painted pale pink. Mum and Gus flew off and left me on the launch pad. As they took off I could hear Gus starting, 'But why can't I go toooo!' The skycar rose higher and as it flew out through the little hatch above, I could hear Gus fading into the distance. 'It's not faaaaaair!' And then they were gone.

When Bianca opened the door I saw she had her hair up and a lot of make-up on. She said, 'Oh, it's you. You're the last one. Everybody's already in the atrium. Come on then. You've met Granny, right?'

'Um, you know I have!' I said.

'Yes, well, whatever, I can't remember exactly who's met her before she had her . . . procedure.' Bianca stopped walking and looked at me properly, for the first time in ages. For a moment she looked like her normal self and she placed her hand on my wrist. 'Granny's had a sort of . . . accident.'

'Oh no!' I said.

Bianca looked down at her feet. 'And since the . . . procedure she's very different, so please don't stare when you meet her.'

'I wouldn't,' I said.

'The thing is, she decided to get some cosmetic surgery to make her look more . . . youthful. She took this serum, but it was the unregulated stuff they make in places like Mars!' Bianca was whispering now. 'The stuff they gave her to make her look young was way too strong and so she looks . . . really, really young.'

'OK.' I nodded, a bit confused.

'Just don't stare and remember she is still an old lady! Be, you know . . . respectful!' said Bianca.

'Of course!' I said.

'She's super-sensitive!' whispered Bianca as we entered a huge room filled with those floating disco lights and the girls from my class. Plus another little girl, about five years old, Gus-sized, her hair cut short and neat, wearing pink lipstick and dressed in a smart suit, pearl earrings and tiny high heels.

'Granny! Here's Lyla!' said Bianca.

The little girl came up to me and shook my hand, saying, 'Ah, yes, Lyla! How lovely to see you again. What a lovely top! Oh my! Those changing colours are simply stunning.'

She had a little girl's voice but she said old lady things. I shook her little hand and said, 'Thank you, Mrs Grimshaw!'

'Oh, really! Do call me "Bianca's granny", we've known each other for quite a while! I hope you have a lot of fun today.' Then she tottered off down a corridor saying, 'I'll just check on that pizza dough, Bianca!'

'It's very hard for her,' whispered Bianca.

We walked down transparent steps into the big atrium where everyone was chewing that gum Amia had bought, smearing that gloss stuff over their lips and throwing the floating disco lights across the big room to each other.

Mercedes had covered her hair in pink glitter. 'Hi, Lyla! Cute top!' she shouted across the room.

Petra looked at me and put her head on one side and said, 'Oh, my goodness! A colour-change top! Those are so over in the Moon Colonies. Is it vintage? I can't believe you still have one!'

I looked up at her and her funny top that was swimming with a moving print of fishes in water making it look like her body was an aquarium. I didn't know what to say, so I just said, 'Nice fish.'

'Yeah, but expensive!!' Then she spun round and said, 'Owen! I need another mocktail!'

Owen, Bianca's big cousin, was there in a black bow tie and white top, pretending to be a waiter. He had a tray of glasses of fizzy drinks and he wandered up to Petra in his socks saying, 'Yes, madam, care for a mocktail?' He's fourteen.

Amia and Mercedes threw the floaty disco lights at his head and giggled.

He offered me a glass so I took one and said, 'Is this champagne?!'

Bianca said, 'Duh, Lyla! It's just a MOCKtail! Elderflower pressé with a bit of lemonade!'

And Owen said in his smarmy deep voice, 'Yeah, I think serving alcohol to eleven-year-olds is like, basically, illegal.'

Everyone laughed as if this was the funniest joke on the planet and Bianca said to Petra, 'I shared a bath with him when I was two! How embarrassing is that?!'

After the mocktails, the throwing disco lights, the giggling and Amia saying, 'Do you have a girlfriend, Owen?' it was time for the pool bit of the party. Bianca's granny's pool is almost as big as the learner pool in the Aquapod in town! Except cleaner.

Everyone changed and Petra did a little model spin in her bikini which was covered with a thousand tiny coloured sparkly beads.

Felicity squealed, 'That's really nice! Are those glass?'

Petra looked down nonchalantly at her shoulder strap. 'Um, no, I think these are crystals. Mum got the bikini for me when we went to the Sea of Tranquillity.'

The pool had a transparent floor. The kitchen is right underneath so Bianca's granny could look up through the water while she was arranging the food and wave her little hand at us.

Bianca said, 'OK! What colour do we want the water?!'

So I said, 'Yellow!'

Bianca pulled a face. 'Like swimming in wee!' For a second I thought we were about to laugh together, but Petra smirked and said, 'Bibi! Let's keep this party sophisticated!'

'Of course!' said Bianca, nervously patting her hair and turning to a voice panel on the wall. 'Purple! Let's have purple!'

The pool water turned purple.

'It's the latest thing, doesn't stain!' Bianca added. 'ONE! TWO! THREE! JUMP!'

Everyone jumped in.

This pool had that special water that doesn't leave you wet; you step out of the water and you're totally dry. Even your hair!

After the pool bit Bianca got really excited and said, 'OK, everyone! We're going to MAKE OUR OWN PIZZA! Like my granny did when she was a girl!'

We had to make these old-fashioned pizza things and put stuff onto them ourselves. With our hands. I thought it was really fun and I could tell Bianca loved it too, but Mercedes said, 'This is gross! It's ruining my nails!' Felicity asked if she could wear some protective gloves.

Bianca's granny laughed. 'Goodness me! We all had to cook for ourselves once. You kids don't know how lucky you are!' which sounded strange coming out of someone who looks five.

Bianca had an aquagro cake, so she dropped the water from the special pipette onto it and we watched it grow from a tiny button thing to this massive cake and then the candles just grow up out of it and finally light themselves.

We sang 'Happy Birthday'.

Then we sang it again because Petra said she could do it with harmonies.

Then Amia said, why don't we put in an extra part, and she and Mercedes did a bit that went, 'Bianca turned eleven and had a party at the Havendome, it was just like heaven!'

Then Petra said, 'So cool! Again! From the top! One, two, three . . .'

Then Bianca's granny said, 'I think someone needs to blow those candles out!'

As we ate the cake Petra said, 'I'm thinking we should all start a girl band! Some of us are really talented! We could practise every break. My dad's got a few contacts in Japan, so he could probably microclone all of us and take the microclones around some pretty big names to get us a record deal. Dad's always travelling.'

Felicity looked up at her all wide-eyed and said, 'Oh, my total gosh! I have always wanted to be in a band!'

'So let's do it!' Petra said, tossing back her hair. 'We could be called *The Crazy Six*! Or *Six Kicks*!'

'But there's seven of us here!' said Bianca, looking at me.

'Oh . . . yeah. Well, we can decide our name later,' said Petra, brushing cake crumbs off her fingers.

Bianca opened my presents first, but she hardly looked at them, pushed the packets aside and said, 'Oh, those . . . thanks.'

Mercedes picked up the stickers and said, 'Oh, those are a total nightmare to get off the walls! My mum can't stand them.'

Then Petra gave Bianca a tub of that hair-growing stuff you can only get in the Moon Colonies.

When Bianca opened it she clutched it to her chest and said, 'This is . . . THE BEST PRESENT OF MY ENTIRE LIFE! LOOK! *Insta-Locks!*'

Petra smiled and said, 'Well, I knew how much you wanted to grow your hair really long, so I asked my dad to get you some last time he was in Catena Yuri!'

'Wait till you see my hair at school on Monday, girls!' said Bianca.

Petra's card had a picture of two teddy bears hugging, inside which she had written:

To my new best friend!
Happy Birthday!
xoxoxoxoxoxoxoxoxo
from Petra!

Bianca said, 'I don't think I really had a proper best friend until this term!'

I said, 'I thought I was.'

It went really quiet, and everybody looked at me

and then at Bianca who said quickly, 'Well, yes, we used to play with each other when we were younger.'

'Yeah, you did! Those stupid Bogwitch games!' laughed Felicity.

While everyone laughed, Petra looked sideways at me and muttered, 'A best friend wouldn't have to get their mummy to beg for an invitation.'

Everyone stopped laughing, no one said a word and I looked down at the bits of cake crumb on my plate.

Bianca's tiny granny bustled in and said, 'Ooh, I say! Are we at a funeral? I don't think I'd be looking gloomy with this pile of presents!'

Bianca smiled and said brightly, 'Yes! So this one is from . . . Franka!'

Franka and Felicity gave Bianca exactly the same set of six iris dyes, that stuff called 'I-Di' that changes your eyes to some crazy colour like bright orange or bright green and it fades after about a month.

Bianca said, 'Two sets! Never mind, I can share some with Petra.'

But Franka said, 'Felicity, how dare you copy my idea!'

And then Felicity looked straight at me and said, 'Well, at least I didn't buy a packet of . . . stickers!'

I was the last person to be collected, the last guest sitting in the big hall with Bianca's tiny granny saying, 'Your mummy does know it ends at six, dear, doesn't she?'

Bianca didn't sit with me. She was in the kitchen laughing with Owen and eating the leftover pizza stuff. Dad came to collect me and he didn't arrive till 6.37!

When Bianca's little granny opened the door he said, 'Oh, hello there!' in a talking-to-babies voice, then he crouched down like you do with little kids and said, 'Do you know who I am? I'm Lyla's daddy. Is there a grown-up here?'

'I am Bianca's grandmother, thank you very much, Mr Hastings! And you are somewhat late,' said Bianca's granny.

'Yes, of course! Sorry! Traffic's unimaginable on the flyway!' said Dad, standing up straight and looking embarrassed.

I said thank you for a nice time, and Bianca's granny said to Dad, 'Such a lovely group of young ladies, all got on so well. Lime Grove is such a friendly school, isn't it?' Then she turned and shouted, 'Bianca! Lyla's going! Come and say goodbye!'

But Bianca didn't bother. She just stopped giggling with her cousin for about two seconds, put her head round the kitchen portal and said, 'Yeah, right, bye.'

Gus was in the skycar. 'What did Bianca think was best – Jelly Gum Bats or Crazee stickers?'

'I don't think she liked any of them much,' I said.

'Why?'

'Got better presents,' I said. 'Like hair-growing stuff.'

'That's not better!' said Gus crossly, then he pressed his nose to the window to count more vehicles on the flyway. 'A Chrysler Comet Intergalactic!' he yelled, making Dad jump. 'They can reach the stratosphere!'

CHAPTER SEVEN

The big news on Monday morning was that Petra and Bianca had used that eye stuff and dyed their eyes with the dye kits from Franka and Felicity. They sat on the wall before school, winking and blinking and opening their eyes wide so everyone could gather round and go, 'Oh wow! Can you squint? Now look to the side!' They had both done one eye orange and one eye purple. The other major event was that Bianca had used the Insta-Locks from Petra and she had come to school with hair so long it trailed on the ground behind her and Louis shouted out in registration, 'Mr Caldwell! Bianca's hair is OUT OF CONTROL! It's a trip hazard!'

'And where has all this new hair come from, Bianca?' said Mr Caldwell. 'I hope you haven't been using any hair-growth products? You do know they are NOT part of school dress code?'

Bianca just looked down.

Then Mr Caldwell said, 'And let me remind you that make-up, including EYE-CHANGING DYE, is also not allowed.'

'Yes, Mr Caldwell,' said Bianca.

'But this stuff takes six weeks to fade,' Felicity pointed out.

Mr Caldwell grunted. 'Well, get that hair trimmed for tomorrow, Bianca!'

We did maths in the morning and Petra said that the use of maths helmets had been stopped in all Moon Colonies. 'I mean, it's hardly improving your brain if you just sit under these stupid metal helmets and all the times tables and stuff just get put into your brain!'

Mr Caldwell didn't tell her off for shouting out like he does if it's Louis. He said, 'Well, yes, even here on Earth there's a lot of discussion about their use.'

At the end of the maths lesson Mr Caldwell said we

should all now have the twelve times table imprinted on our minds.

Louis said, 'Don't know about the twelve times table but I've got this maths helmet stuck on my head! Pull me out, James!'

'LOUIS! Careful! That's expensive equipment!' said Mr Caldwell. 'Oh yes, that reminds me, this break you and Lyla can polish the maths helmets, as agreed, after your awful behaviour on the trip last week.'

So we did, using the special spray. Miss Fritz came in to check on our progress, and said, 'Keep . . . Up . . . Up . . . the good . . . work . . . nice. Nice. UP!' Then she turned and went.

Louis said, 'In my cousin's school they've got the proper ones that look like real people. They had to have about fifty cake sales to buy them, though!'

· ✳·⭐.✳ *

This was the first time I'd been in trouble enough to miss a break since the wedding business with Bianca and James in Year Two.

'You're kidding me!' said Louis. 'I miss break all the

time. I'll be missing it again when they see what I did with the playground weather settings! Ha!'

But he couldn't tell me what he'd done to them because suddenly all the girls had gathered outside the window by our classroom and Petra was making them sing that Moon Colonies song really LOUDLY!

'Give it all you've GOT!' she was yelling. 'Franka, I need to see MORE emotion!'

Louis put one of the polished maths helmets on his head to block out the sound and I suddenly remembered . . . it was a band rehearsal!

I went over and knocked on the window and said, 'I'll COME AT LUNCH TIME!'

But Petra just folded her arms, looked at me all furious and mouthed, 'LIKE I CARE!'

By lunch time the playground was full of snow, thanks to Louis messing with the weather settings. Mr Caldwell was furious, but he soon found out who was responsible as Louis had spent the first five minutes in the playground shouting, 'SNOW! I BRING YOU SNOW! DON'T ALL THANK ME AT ONCE!'

Mr Caldwell said this was a serious misuse of school property and Louis was to go straight to the head teacher, Mrs Fradley. Mr Caldwell continued, 'You have also inconvenienced all the other students!'

Louis shrugged and just said, 'What's the big problem, Mr C? Look at them! Snowballs everywhere! I've done them a favour! Look at that lot over there!'

Over by the real bushes a bunch of Year Twos were hurling snowballs over the perimeter fence and shouting, 'Bogwitch! Have a snowball! Wash your stinky face with it!' They were clapping and laughing. Miss Fritz was shuffling towards them, so they ran away from the fence, back into the Infant Zone, kicking up snow with their feet as they went.

Mr Caldwell continued talking to Louis but I'd stopped listening. I was just feeling the cool flakes of snow falling on my face and watching how the snow had started to settle on the top of the perimeter fence and dust the leaves of the real bushes.

'And what do you think of Louis' behaviour, Lyla?' said Mr Caldwell.

'I like snow,' I said quietly.

Louis turned back and gave me a little thumbs up as Mr Caldwell took him off to see Mrs Fradley. I put my tongue out to taste the flakes of snow and as I stood there, all alone. I saw a snowball come flying back over the perimeter fence! I couldn't be sure, so I walked closer to the spot where it had fallen into the smooth snow.

A snowball. Thrown from the other side. And thrown hard. An *angry* snowball! So there really was someone or something living over there!

I had to tell Bianca!

I ran over to the other girls. I ran through the snow, all excited and breathing fast. When I got to the other side of the playground Petra was standing on the little wall so she could conduct band practice. She was waving her arms about like she was conducting a big orchestra.

'I'm here! For the rehearsal!' I said, and waved up at her. 'And, Bianca! Guess what?! We were right! There really *is* someone living over the perimeter fence. We didn't just make it up! They just threw a snowball over the fence. I saw it! I'll show you where it landed!'

They all stopped singing and Petra looked down at me from the wall. 'What are you even talking about? Could you just shut up? Some of us have a rehearsal!' She turned back to the others and said, 'OK! Even in snow, we practise! The Six Sensations are ready to rock!'

'Well, it's The *Seven* Sensations 'cause I'm here now,' I said.

Petra got down off the wall and came very close to me, so close I could see right into her new orange and purple eyes. 'The Six Sensations sounds better!' she hissed right into my face.

'And we'd probably sound better without you!' said Felicity.

'You're not mature enough,' said Franka.

'You did miss the first rehearsal,' said Mercedes quietly.

'You did,' said Bianca, even more quietly, looking down and shifting the snow about with her foot.

'You DID!' said Petra. 'And you're a babyish troublemaker who hangs out with Louis and TOTALLY interrupts us, going *blah blah I saw someone with a snowball blah di blah!* Who cares anyway? Why don't you just leave us alone? When will you understand that no one likes you! No one! You stupid little . . . Earthling!'

I turned and walked away.

'Lyla!' shouted Bianca. 'Wait!'

I had that tight feeling in my throat that means you might cry. I walked through the snow and through all the little kids throwing snowballs. I felt hot wet tears about to tip down my face so I screwed my eyes up tight to try and squeeze them back in.

Bianca had started to walk through the snow to catch me up. Petra was following with all the others but I ran behind the flyke sheds.

'Leave her, Bianca!' shouted Petra. 'We haven't got time for this!'

But they were all still walking my way.

Franka shouted so I could hear, 'I bet she's crying too!'

Soon I had crossed right to the edge of the playground where the squishy floor reaches the big metal perimeter fence, which you can't even see over, as it's so high. The old Bogwitch corner. I was hidden by the bushes and now I was properly crying with those big gulps. So I kept staring hard at the perimeter fence and fiddling with the edge of one of the panels, whispering to myself, 'Stop crying, please stop crying!'

As I ran my fingers along the edge of the smooth grey panel I noticed that this panel had lost a few of its bolts. I could slip my fingers under it.

And with not much pulling I made a gap!

CHAPTER EIGHT

The other girls were just behind the bushes. They had stopped walking and I could hear Bianca saying, 'But we don't have to be so . . . mean!'

'Petra's not being mean! She's just telling her the truth,' said Franka.

'Exactly!' said Petra. 'Where did she go? She needs to grow up and apologise right now for ruining this rehearsal!'

Sometimes a gap looks really narrow, but you can still squeeze through if you turn sideways and you're small for your year. So I did. Squeezing myself away from Moon Girl!

Once through, I closed the gap quickly, wiped the

snot and tears off my face with my sleeve and looked around a wild overgrown place.

It was an old-style garden, full of real trees and bushes.

I could hear them on the other side. 'OK, she's not here, so she's probably hiding in the flyke sheds! And I am so not about to play hide-and-seek!' said Petra. 'Come on, let's go sing!'

Their voices began to fade as they ran back to rehearse.

On the other side of the perimeter fence it was nothing like how Bianca and I had imagined it in our Bogwitch game. It was so odd to be in a place we'd imagined for years but never seen. I wanted to find all the things we'd put on Bianca's old maps and drawings. I know it's silly, but I felt kind of disappointed! It was all just weeds and tall grass, no Tower of the Mighty Bogwitch, no death pit. I walked on through the high bushes, catching my clothes on brambles and branches.

As I made my way up the garden it became a little less overgrown and there was a broken glass house thing, real old glass! My feet crunched over the bits.

I've never seen real glass. I wanted to pick some up to look at, but I've heard it's so dangerous I didn't. Actually I was getting a bit worried about it under my shoes, so I got up on a low stone wall by some stone steps. Now I was standing a bit higher up I could see over the bushes and right up to the top of the garden. I could see the back of a really ancient house with a pointy roof, old chimney, no launch pad and a rusty old wind generator, like the ones they preserved in that Yesterday Village place.

I carried on walking up the garden. It wasn't snowing any more, as I was out of the playground weather system, far, far away from Moon Girl.

Then I heard something, like a baby's cry only . . . scary. Something furry darted out of the bushes and brushed past my leg. I could hear my own heartbeat! I looked down and there was a much larger version of Sparks looking up at me and doing the scary, meowy noise.

I clapped my hands and said, 'Bedtime, Sparks!'

But instead of falling asleep in a tidy ball of fur, this massive cat thing jumped up from the ground. Up into a branch of a tree, level with my head! We were eye to eye.

I didn't move.

I've heard about real cats. They're very dangerous — they hunt and kill things. And sometimes they kill things just for fun!

So I stayed completely still while it looked right at me. I thought I might be stuck looking into a ferocious cat's eyes for ever, but then something else came through the grasses and bushes. Somebody was coming down the garden, shouting, 'Fluffy Tums! Fluffy Tums!'

The cat decided to stay on the branch and carry on staring me out with its evil green eyes.

The voice was really close now. 'Hey! Fluffy Tums! Where are you?'

I shouted out, 'Here!'

An old woman came crashing out of the bushes, hardly taller than me, holding a saucer of cat food. She was probably in her hundreds but she moved quickly. She wore a jumble of ancient clothes and her feet were in shoes with stringy laces trailing in the mud – trainers, like Mercedes had worn to Yesterday Village. She wore a pair of moonshades, but they were on wonky and she had tried to mend them with some tape.

She didn't look pleased to see me. 'You had me thinking Fluffy Tums had learned to talk!' she said.

She put the food down on the floor and came up very close to my face. I could see there were two tiny little cats curled up and sleeping in the huge mass of her white hair: her hair was a nest for kittens!

She blinked at me through the smeary lenses of the moonshades, her bright eyes looking right into mine. 'I don't need this! No, sir,' she said crossly. 'I've had stray cats, foxes, rats, bats and squirrels coming into this garden. But I am not welcoming STRAY GIRLS! No, sir!'

'Sorry!' I said. 'I came through the perimeter fence! There's a loose panel, sorry, I'll go!'

'You better!' she said. 'This is private land! I've had nasty little kids banging on my fence with sticks for years! Most days I don't go anywhere near the fence – I can't. Those little so-and-sos throw stuff over! I keep quiet and I can ignore the disgusting things they shout. But sneaking into MY private garden? No, sir! I can't ignore that. No way! You can shoo right off. Go on! Out! OUT!'

I started walking back down the garden towards the fence, still scared that Fluffy Tums might launch a deadly attack. But just as I was about to squeeze out and back into the playground, she called out, 'Hey, girl! You know what? As you're here . . . got any experience fixing . . . short-range passenger rockets?'

I turned round and said, 'Um . . . no.'

She pushed the old moonshades up her nose. 'Well, I'm guessing you could hold a ladder while I climb up it, keep it steady?'

'I could, but lunch break will be over in twenty minutes!'

'Long enough, follow me!'

We made our way back up the overgrown garden. The old woman knew exactly where to duck down, and as she bent low or pushed past a branch, those two little kittens stayed sleeping in the nest of her hair.

'I like your kittens,' I said, trying to be friendly.

'Yeah, I'm bringing them up as my own now their mum, Shadow, died last month. Great cat, always there for me . . . know what I mean?' She paused to wipe a tear from her eye on the back of her sleeve,

'Crazy how much I miss that old girl!'

'You talk about her like she was a person,' I said.

'No. I talk about her like she was a cat. Cats are better than people. People suck.'

We were almost up to the house when she turned round and said, 'Now, I don't want you going around blabbing about me. I'm a very secretive person, keep myself to myself. Got it?'

I nodded.

'The thing is, I used to be an astronaut, kind of big back then, one of the first Mars Pioneers, the first mission in 2078. But when they make you this big-time celebrity it's chat shows, autographs, fans sitting on your doorstep! "Hey! What did you eat for breakfast?" Idiots, they drive you crazy! People, I'm sick of them. But I've still got the rocket, love the rocket!'

'Wow!' I said.

'Never mind "Wow"! Don't go blabbing!'

We came to a clearing right next to the house and there was this old rusty rocket thing. It looked out of place next to all the broken flowerpots and old garden furniture. The old lady began walking round it, picking up tools, checking her little kittens were still safe in her hair and kicking old bits of metal out of her way.

'Yeah, I need to get flying again, want to take trips to the Moon, shops are better in Catena Yuri, but something's up with the hydrogen cell. Can't afford to pay for it to be fixed. Been grounded for about ten years. Driving me crazy! Feel like a bird without wings!'

She got me to hold the bottom of a ladder she had propped up beside the rocket while she began climbing.

Halfway up she looked down at me. 'Remember, you don't tell anyone about this, got it? Don't want your little pals coming in here. I'm not a people person. I'm only allowing you in here 'cause you can hold a ladder better than a cat. Don't tell your friends!'

'I haven't got any.' I shrugged.

'Sensible girl,' she muttered. 'Now pass me that spanner.'

After a few minutes with the old lady banging about above me, I heard Miss Fritz on her playground duty: 'ALERT! Lunch . . . OVER. ALERT!'

'I have to go!' I called.

'Yeah, yeah! OK!' the old lady shouted impatiently, coming down the ladder. She was a little out of breath as she reached the ground. 'Not fixed yet, there's more to do!'

'But I have to go,' I said, and I started to walk back down the garden, dodging branches again.

The old woman followed me and watched as I started to squeeze through the gap.

'I better get that fixed too!' she said. 'Stop any more nosy little trespassers!'

'Yes,' I said. 'Don't worry, I won't bother you again!'

I pushed the loose panel forward just enough to squish myself through and I was almost back into the playground, just getting my head through the gap without grazing my nose, when she said, 'I'm thinking . . . could you come again? Not to see me, just . . . to . . . you know, hold the ladder? So I can get that piece of junk fixed?'

'Maybe!' I smiled.

Back in the playground I pushed the panel back in place and tried to do a quick run-walk thing, without looking too suspicious, back to the class hub. The teachers had turned off the snow.

It was PE that afternoon in the Low Gravity Centre. It's a massive room you go into in your socks and PE suits. No bare feet allowed, as the cleaning bots don't want sweaty footmarks up the walls. When everyone is in, Mr Caldwell presses buttons and you start to float, and when it's zero gravity you can do all these somersaults like they do in space. It's so you can be prepared if you ever want to work as an engineer on a Mars Mission when you grow up, like I do. I'm not good at normal sport, but I am good at low gravity.

Before he turned on the zero gravity, Mr Caldwell folded his arms and said, 'Remember, if anyone is caught doing dangerous fast moves they will not be visiting the Low Gravity Centre in the foreseeable future!'

Petra said, 'Mr Caldwell, I've spent eleven years in low gravity! Can I sit this out?'

Mr Caldwell said, 'We all do PE, Petra! It's a chance for you to demonstrate some of your advanced skills to the class.'

Well, Petra didn't seem to have any advanced skills. She just swished her hair about, saying, 'Does this look like a shampoo advert?' to Franka and Felicity.

Once we'd settled into floating about, Mr Caldwell got out the low-gravity equipment so we could practise our manual skills for life in space.

I love it! I am the only person who has never let a spanner zoom off, and Mr Caldwell sometimes gets me to demonstrate the new things first to the class. I wish

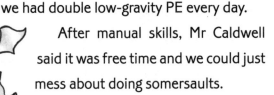

we had double low-gravity PE every day.

After manual skills, Mr Caldwell said it was free time and we could just mess about doing somersaults.

As I did a backflip I saw a piece of paper float out of Petra's pocket. She tried to catch it but it floated away. It came near enough for me to reach out and grab it.

A MOON GIRL STOLE MY FRIEND

It was a list written in Petra's curly handwriting:

Five great reasons NOT to talk to Lyla Hastings!!!!!

1. STUPID hair! Hahahaha
2. LOVES Louis! YUCK!
3. IMMATURE!!!!! e.g. likes stickers!
4. Cannot sing
5. Boring i.e. NOT FASHIONABLE

And at the bottom it said:

> Signed by THE SIX SENSATIONS!
>
> Petra Lumen
>
> Franka Thornton
>
> Felicity Phillips
>
> Amia Diaz
>
> Mercedes Bonnay

I felt kind of sick, floating there, I looked at it again. Only five names . . . Bianca hadn't signed.

I pushed myself off the wall so I could shoot right back to Petra and said, 'Oh, lost this?!'

'That's private!' she snapped, trying to snatch it from me.

I ripped it up into tiny pieces right under her nose. The pieces floated everywhere!

I'd forgotten about the low gravity and Mr Caldwell shouted, 'WHO did that!? IT WILL BLOCK THE FILTERS!' and turned off the low gravity so fast we all came down with a crash.

The second we landed Petra said, 'Lyla! It was Lyla! Who else would be so stupid?!'

At the end of the day I walked into the coatpod and all of them were there, singing their Six Sensations songs while they got their coats. The second I walked in they all stopped and stared at me, especially Petra.

I got my coat, ignoring them.

Then Louis barged through us saying, 'Move, ladies! Home time! I'm outta here!'

James Defries followed him, walking through the silent, staring girls. He cupped his hand behind his ear and said, 'Wow, this is great! What can I hear? NO SINGING! No offence, but take it from me, you need waaaay more practice with that singing stuff!'

Louis ran out of the portal, laughing and saying, 'Not wrong there, mate! They sound like the brakes on my flyke!'

They ran off across the playground together, doing bad impersonations of The Six Sensations. Louis was doing a stupid dance and singing, 'Ooh la la! I need a bra!'

'Idiots!' said Petra. 'What do they know about music?!'

I walked out of the coatpod after the boys. I had to step over Petra's foot because she wouldn't pull it in as I walked past her.

No one said bye to me.

No one said anything.

CHAPTER NINE

I tried to talk to Mum about the no one-talking-to-me situation on the way to school next morning, but the traffic was busy on the flyway and she kept tutting and saying things like, 'Thanks! Don't bother to indicate!' to the other skycars above us. As we began flying down onto the school launch pad she said, 'They can't all be that bad! Bianca's a great girl!'

'She was,' I whispered to no one, and looked up at the clouds and the flying skycars.

Gus leaned over and stuck his face right in front of mine. 'I know! GREAT IDEA! You can be best friends with ME and Evan! We're very nice. WE talk all the time!'

'I know,' I said.

Gus went on excitedly, 'We can play Moon Wars together! We need someone to be a Moon Defence marshal in our game! Today!'

'Thanks, Gus, I'll think about it.'

'You need to chase us about and pretend to track us down! You'll really like it! Probably be the best playtime of your life!'

'Maybe,' I said.

I walked over to the portals of the coatpod slowly. When I walked in, all the girls were standing about discussing whether Bianca should grow her hair again with the Insta-Locks.

Bianca was saying, 'I really liked the extra length but obviously I had to get it shorter again for school.'

'You could always use the Insta-Locks in the summer break,' said Petra.

I shoved my coat into my suction hatch and said, 'But it did look a bit weird that long.'

'Like anyone asked for your opinion!' said Felicity, folding her arms.

Petra looked at Felicity, all angry, and said, 'Felicity! What did we agree?! Lyla isn't worth talking to!'

They fell silent and just watched me walk off into the class hub.

I heard Petra whisper, 'Talking of hair, did you see Lyla's? That girl has zero style!'

Felicity tittered.

Next lunch break Petra pushed past me as she and the others went out into the playground. She didn't say sorry — she didn't even look at me. She was too busy tossing her hair about and telling everyone how she had decided to move the rehearsals.

'Look, we can't focus with stupid boys listening to our practice sessions! We're professionals. We need privacy and I was thinking the launch pad is always empty at break. We can sing up there.'

'You're so clever!' said Felicity. 'No one goes right up there at break.'

'Exactly – it's high up and deserted! We won't have anyone judging us or putting us off. Plus, my dad's off to Japan in two weeks and could take microclones of us singing out there to show all the really big shot people. We don't have time to waste. Come on, to the launch pad!'

And off they ran, giggling, to the launch pad, running up the steps that spiral up round the outside. It's one of the oldest parts of Lime Grove Edu Hub. The launch pad is really close to the staff room. The steps are so close to the staff-room portal I was amazed Miss Fritz hadn't told them to stop singing up there while the teachers had their coffee. But like Louis says, Miss Fritz is a bit old and slow.

I walked over to the wall that's between our playground and the little Infant Zone playground so I could see Gus. Maybe I *should* join him. Maybe playing Moon Wars with a bunch of Year One boys would be fun? He had loads of little boys with him, all running around and shouting stuff.

Gus was in charge. 'OK, guys! Think strategy! Neutron Defence Shields on!' He didn't look like someone who sticks penguin stickers all over his tummy. He looked more grown-up.

And he looked popular.

I stood for a few more minutes looking at him and wishing I could go back in time to Year One when it was just me and Bianca having fun. But there was nothing for me to do in this playground any more so I walked slowly right over to the perimeter fence, to where that loose panel was. Two little girls saw me and said in that small girl singsong voice, 'Mrs Fradley doesn't let anyone touch the fence and it's a rule.'

'I know,' I said, and waited till they'd gone. Then I felt the edge of the panel.

She hadn't fixed it!

As soon as I had squeezed inside, Fluffy Tums brushed past my legs. I froze. But he looked up at me and curled his tail about my leg. He didn't look too scary so I bent down very slowly to pat his back. He made a little growly sound so I pulled my hand back quickly.

I walked up towards the house and came to the clearing. There was the rocket and there was the old woman, talking to herself and walking about with a bucket of soapy water and an old rag. She was trying to clean the curved sides of the rocket; dirty water slopped onto the floor.

I did a little, 'Hello?'

She turned quickly, like a startled squirrel. 'Here again?'

'Well, you hadn't fixed the fence and, um, you did say I should maybe come back and hold the ladder?'

'I did? I was probably just being polite!' she shouted, and turned back to her careless cleaning with the wet rag. 'Anyway, no need, it's all fixed! You can buzz off. I'm busy today, about to take this up for a test flight!' She turned back to face me and flapped her wet hands at me like she was shooing away an insect. 'I saw enough of you yesterday!'

I didn't say anything. And I didn't move. I looked down at the rough grass.

She came towards me and looked at me with her head on one side. 'A real sad, stray girl, aren't you?'

'I am a bit . . . sad,' I said. 'I really don't think I have any friends any more.'

'You and me both!' She smiled. 'Here, hold a kitten – they make everything better!' She put her hand up into her big hair and pulled out one of the tiny kittens and placed it into my hand. 'That's Baby Shadow and this' – she pulled out the second – 'is Little Smokey. You got a pet?'

'Only a cybercat, not a real one.'

I looked at the tiny kittens' big eyes and their little ears on the side of their heads. So soft and warm! Baby Shadow made little snuffly noises as she licked my fingers. 'They have pink tongues! Sparks' tongue is blue!'

'Cyberpets, huh, they're no good. All wires inside. No heart. Let's put these two darlings in their day bed and see if we can take this thing up!' She kicked the rocket. 'You want to come? Quick trip to outer space?'

'But lunch break's only—'

'Twenty minutes, yeah, yeah, I remember! So we'll just get it up above the house and test the basics. Come on! Oh, bring that oil can there, need to oil the passenger hatch!'

My hands got covered in the black oil.

'So what? Wipe it on your trousers!' said the old woman. 'What's a bit of oil? When I was all those years in space I didn't go fretting about oil stains!'

'But it's my school clothes,' I said.

She ignored me and began climbing up into the rocket. 'This is quite a small rocket, it's only a two-seater, so you go on the left with the main controls!'

'I can't fly a rocket!'

'You don't know till you try. Come on! Seatbelt on! Quick! You're the one who's only got twenty minutes.'

It was all a bit messy inside the passenger compartment. There were cat hairs everywhere and old sweet packets lying about. 'Did you take cats up into space?' I asked.

'Sure, they loved it! And if we've fixed this right they'll be up again! Right, so press this, then that!'

I followed her instructions and the rocket burst into loud, juddering sounds. I was a bit scared, but excited too. 'Is that how it's supposed to sound?'

The old woman sighed. 'It's sounded better, but look, we're going up! We did it! It's working!'

We rose above the pointy roof of the house and took a slow little journey above the garden. Compared to our skycar, the rocket felt like a powerful old monster finding it hard to get up into the air. I could see right across the playground and even make out Bianca and Petra and the others doing dance moves on top of the launch pad.

'Look where you're going! You can't be staring out at the view! You'll have my chimney off! OK, that's enough. I need to fine-tune it a bit before I go any further. Let's bring it down!'

We landed back by the house. The old woman got out first and slid down the side of the rocket to get to the ground. 'Darn it! You landed on my plant pots!

At about your age I could fly like a professional – you modern kids don't know any of the old skills!'

'Sorry!' I said, sliding down the side of the rocket after her. 'Lucky I didn't squash a cat!'

'My clever cats know to get out of the way!' she said, picking up the two little kittens from their day bed and putting them back into her hair very gently. She smiled at me. 'Actually, you weren't that bad, for a kid. How old are you?'

'Ten.' And then I babbled on, 'Young for my year but I'm always the best in low gravity. Maybe I have natural flying skills! I play flying on my Float 'n' Sleep. That's probably why I did such a great first try!'

The old woman laughed. 'Broken plant pots is not "a great first try", but you'll get better.'

I heard Miss Fritz doing her playground round-up. 'I have to go! Thanks for the rocket lesson!'

'Yes, well, remember – pilots need to focus!' she said, going back to washing the rocket with the dirty water. But as I walked down the garden, she called after me, 'You got a name?'

'Lyla!' I shouted.

'Mine's Betty Astral!' she called back. 'But don't you tell anyone about me! I'm a very private person! Got it?'

'Got it!' I yelled back.

I started to run but Betty called out again, 'Hey, Lyla, come and see me again? Well, not to see me, just help . . . with the rocket. It's always best to take a co-pilot on a high-altitude test flight, especially at my age, just while I'm getting that old thing back up to speed.'

'I'm not really allowed,' I yelled back. 'But I'll try!'

'Yeah, try!' she shouted back down the garden.

When I got to the end of the garden Miss Fritz was right there, on the other side, saying, 'I. detect life . . . forms. Any. One. Here?'

So I kept still.

Then Miss Fritz said, 'No life forms. Detected. Returning to basic . . . playground duties.' I had to wait while she shuffled all the way back across the playground.

I was so late Mr Caldwell had already started afternoon lessons and everyone was labelling a diagram of a leaf.

'Nice of you to join us, Lyla!' said Mr Caldwell angrily. 'The lunch break finished ten minutes ago! Where have you been?'

I didn't have time to think so I said, 'The personal hygiene vaporisers! Sorry!'

'Really, and can you explain the . . . mud? The . . . what is it . . . oil?'

The class giggled.

I looked down at my oil-stained hands from the rocket, and muddy knees from crawling under the bushes.

'Perhaps you should go back to the personal hygiene vaporisers and clean some of that off!' Mr Caldwell barked.

When I finally sat down behind Bianca she looked back at me, gave me a tiny smile and whispered, 'What happened?!'

'Tell you another time!' I murmured back.

Then Petra jabbed Bianca so hard she was shoved sideways. 'Ow!' said Bianca, turning to glare at Petra. 'That really hurt!'

'So?! What did we all agree, Bianca? We don't talk to her. Look at her! Covered in mud and sitting in persovaps all day long!' hissed Petra. 'She's like a toddler!'

CHAPTER TEN

The next day I stood behind Louis in the lunch queue. We got our trays and were taking our food from the lunch supervisor bots. The Six Sensations were already on a table with their lunches. Usually these days they would be doing annoying 'vocal warm-ups' that Petra made them do every day. She made them go 'Mee mee mee! Laa laa laa!' while they ate their jellyfish crispies. And one of the old lunch supervisor bots would come over and say, 'Lunch time is for eating,' and they'd stop singing, but just until the bot had rolled back to the serving hatches.

But this lunch time they weren't singing. They were having a massive argument.

Louis turned round and said to me, 'World War Four breaking out on the blue table!'

I looked over and saw that Franka was crying and saying, 'Petra! You lied! You said he had proper contacts with people in Japan!' Snot and tears were falling onto her plate. 'You totally lied!'

'I didn't,' Petra was saying, with her arms folded across her chest.

'YOU DID!' shouted Mercedes, almost knocking over her yoghurt. 'You said your dad could get us made up as microclones and everything and get us a record deal!'

'I said he *might*!' said Petra.

'Well, now we've wasted all that time practising our songs for NOTHING!' said Felicity.

'We can still put all our stuff out there like everyone else does, we don't need the microclones,' said Bianca.

'Exactly,' said Petra.

Louis and I walked past their table carrying our trays.

'But I'm so DISAPPOINTED!' wailed Felicity. 'I had my heart set on being a STAR!'

So then everyone gathered round to comfort her.

Except Petra, who stood up at the end of the table

with her hands on her hips, saying, 'Oh come on! Stop being so babyish and let's carry on rehearsing. Maybe I can get us a show on Catena Yuri through my old modelling contacts.'

'But you were only a baby then!' laughed Bianca.

Petra looked at her and said, 'So what? At least I've actually done something with my life – unlike *you*, Bianca! All you've ever done is cover your whole room with stupid walking penguin stickers! Come on! To the launch pad!'

And they all got up and went out to the playground. I watched them through the big window walking over to the launch pad, Petra striding out in front and the others dragging along behind.

I got up too, and decided to go straight to Betty's. I was getting good at doing an inconspicuous stroll over to the fence, and this time I slipped through the fence easily, knowing just when to turn my head and pull the panel shut behind me without a sound.

I walked back up the garden and found Betty sitting in the sun by the rocket, trying to get the little kittens to eat their food out of an old china dish without them walking through it. She looked up at me and smiled. 'Well, just the person I was hoping might come by!' She stood up and kicked the rocket with her foot. 'Want to do a bit of high-altitude work?'

'Won't that take longer than my lunch break?' I said.

'Two minutes to go about two hundred miles up, admire the view, and in this little old beauty, probably ten minutes back down!'

The little rocket rose like a tired old monster again.

Betty let me do the controls, but she also did a lot of yelling: 'Whoa, less wrist-wobbling, Lyla!' Sometimes she just grabbed the controls off me. But as we went up I started to feel more a part of the rocket, more like I do just doing my flips in the Low Gravity Centre.

Betty patted my hand as I held the controls. 'Nice work! Took me quite a few months to get that pitching under control, and you've done it in minutes!'

'Am I good?' I asked, turning to her.

'You will be if you keep your eyes ahead!'

Once we were high above the Earth we turned off the power so we could admire the beautiful blue seas under the swirl of clouds.

'There's a view you never get sick of!' sighed Betty. 'You been this high before?'

'When I was four we had a summer holiday in New Zealand and we went by shuttle, but I was too scared to look out of the windows then,' I said, pressing my face close to the window. 'The Moon still looks so far away! That's where Petra's from.'

'And who's this Petra?' asked Betty. 'Said you didn't have any friends.'

So I told her about Petra. *All* about Petra. Right up to the quarrel in the dining hall. 'Is it 'cause she's from the Moon? Is that why she's just so mean?' I wondered.

'No, there are mean girls all over this galaxy!' laughed Betty. 'Trust me, I've met them! Mean girls, mean boys, mean everybodies! Don't worry too much about what those girls think, Lyla. Be yourself and you'll find true friends. You only need a couple or so. Heck, I've only got one cat and two kittens and that's enough friends for me!'

'Really?' I said.

'Maybe,' said Betty, looking a little sad.

We sat in silence, gazing out at the stars.

Betty looked far up into space. 'For the most part Moonites are nice people, if a bit flashy. I've met a few aliens up there on my missions too – they're OK, I guess, but they're some of the worst drivers! Fly anywhere they like!' She turned on the ignition again. 'Come on, we better get you down!'

I practically landed the rocket on my own! Apart from Betty shrieking, 'LANDING GEAR! NOW!' in my ear, I think I did quite a good job.

'Well, that was interesting!' said Betty. 'Out you get!'

As I climbed out of the rocket and slid down the side I said, 'Betty . . .'

'Betty . . . what?' she said from the cockpit.

I stood on the ground and looked up at her, 'Thanks for the trip. It was great and . . .'

'And . . . ?' she said impatiently.

'Will anybody talk to me ever again?' I said.

'I'm talking to you!'

'No . . . the girls.'

'Trust me, they can't keep it up for ever! I've lived long enough to know that not one thing stays the same in this universe. Something will change – you, them, the weather! Now, if you'll excuse me, this little rocket seems to be in perfect condition so I've got to get up to Catena Yuri for some blue bananas. You need anything?'

'No, thanks.'

She started up the rocket.

'Bye!' I waved up to her. 'Can I visit again? Even now the rocket's fixed?'

'Well, you're not as nice as a cat! But almost . . . so yeah, why not?!' She winked at me and started firing up the jets.

I ran down the garden, suddenly realising I'd spent way too long chatting to Betty. I was in such a mad rush I didn't even check before I squished through the fence and ran straight into . . . Miss Fritz!

Miss Fritz wobbled and assessed the situation, her big, fake eyes scanning the gap in the fence and then scanning me.

'Serious incident. Pupil has left school grounds. SERIOUS INCIDENT. Must report to. Head teacher. Please follow. Me. Lyla.'

I walked beside her, saying, 'Do you have to report it, miss? I'm in trouble all the time! I promise I won't go out ever again.'

But you can't negotiate with a cyborg playground supervisor. Miss Fritz just shuffled her way towards Mrs Fradley's office, saying, 'SERIOUS INCIDENT. Must report. Offender Lyla Hastings.'

Mrs Fradley sat behind her smooth white desk and looked at me. 'I'm disappointed, Lyla! And Mr Caldwell says your behaviour has deteriorated this term. You must promise you will never – and I mean NEVER – leave the school premises during a school day again! Is that clear?'

I nodded.

She said I'd be missing lunch-time break for a whole week! She had to call my parents.

That afternoon, as I walked across the playground to go home, I heard footsteps running up behind me.

It was Bianca, smiling, 'Lyla! Wait! What did you DO? It's all round school!'

But Petra and the others then caught up with us and Petra said, 'Oh, like anyone cares what she did! Stupid Earthling!'

Felicity gave a little nervous titter.

Bianca said very quietly, 'You shouldn't really say stuff like that, Petra. And we don't say *Earthling* — it's . . . a bit . . . well, we don't say it.'

Everyone else just looked down at their feet. I walked on.

Gus was so cross with me about being in massive trouble he wouldn't even look at me when I got into the skycar. But Mum didn't stop going on and on about it! All the way home!

'But what were you THINKING!? Leaving school grounds! And hiding behind the perimeter fence!'

I hadn't said anything about Betty or the rocket.

The story was that I'd just gone the one time to sit at the bottom of an old garden, but this still made me either 'Seriously weird!' according to James, or 'A total jelly bat who shouldn't ever, ever have started playing with bad Louis!' according to Gus.

I thought it would be harder to adjust to being an official bad child, but missing breaks all the time doesn't mean much when you don't have any real friends. Plus, Louis was there most of the lunch-time breaks that week and then James had to stay in on the Thursday, because he had kicked a football up on the Low Gravity Centre roof and to get it down he went up there by sitting on a window-cleaning bot that was working its way up the windows to the roof.

'I don't see the problem!' James was telling us. 'Those cleaning bots are just machines, little square things. I thought it was a great idea! Sat on the bot and got a lift up! But Mr Caldwell was all: "*We have to respect the cyborg community and not sit on top of them when we fancy a lift.*" But cleaning bots aren't cyborgs! It's not like I sat on Miss Fritz's head and asked *her* to carry me anywhere!'

Miss Fritz came in then to see how we were getting on with our job of folding up all the 3D Galaxy maps and sorting the geography shelf. She came in very slowly. If a cyborg can look tired, she did.

'How. Going? Foldy . . . maps?' she said, her voice even slower than usual.

'Good, thanks!' I said.

'How. Going? Folda?' she repeated.

Louis, James and I looked at each other and James said, very loudly and clearly, 'It's going well! Very well! All good! We are folding the maps!'

Miss Fritz's head tilted to one side and her big eyes closed for a second. It looked like she was about to topple over.

Louis got up from his seat and went over to her. 'MISS FRITZ! CAN YOU HEAR ME? I THINK YOU NEED TO GO AND RECHARGE! YOU'RE NOT LOOKING WELL!'

Miss Fritz lifted her head up and opened her eyes and said, 'LOW BATTERY ALERT.'

'Yes, that's probably it,' said Louis, now taking her hand and leading her to the portal. He pushed her gently towards the staff room. 'You go and have a nice little rest.'

We watched her wobbling down the corridor to the staff room.

'I feel sorry for her,' I said.

'Why?' said James. 'She's just an old electrical appliance! That's like feeling sorry for a fridge!'

I looked up from my pile of maps and saw the girls running off to do their band practice up on the launch pad. They were all linking arms and laughing. It was a clear, cold, sunny day out there.

'Is that the real weather?' I asked. 'Or playground setting weather?'

'Real weather!' said Louis. 'Because it's everywhere.'

We didn't talk for a bit; we just sorted the geography stuff. Then there was an ear-shattering siren.

'Fire drill?' said James. 'Brilliant! No more folding! Come on!'

'Fire drill? In a lunch break?' I said.

Mr Caldwell suddenly put his head round the portal. 'Out, you three! Quick! Quick! Fire alarm!'

CHAPTER ELEVEN

In a fire drill we all go to the zones where each class has to line up. I was thinking that lunch break is a waste of a fire drill, even when you're folding maps. It's better if it's in something like maths.

The teachers started checking everyone was there. Mr Caldwell was just beginning to count our class and then Mrs Fradley came out. Now, usually Mrs Fradley comes out and walks about at the front of everyone all lined up and says, 'Not bad, Lime Grove! Two minutes twenty-seven seconds!'

But this time she ran! She ran straight to Mr Caldwell and said, 'Not a drill! Whole staff room on fire! Emergenbots have been called! Nightmare! Miss Fritz overheated, her hair caught alight and . . . OH! OH! LOOK AT THE SMOKE!'

Turns out that our head teacher is NOT calm under pressure. She didn't walk calmly up and down like she does in the drill – she ran about all over the place yelling, 'STAFF! IS EVERY CHILD ACCOUNTED FOR?!'

The smoke swirled up into the blue sky. We all stood in our lines.

Then Mr Caldwell said, 'I'M MISSING SIX!'

Mrs Fradley clutched her head and said, 'Where are those emergenbots! Who exactly is missing, Mr Caldwell?!'

He read out the names: Franka, Felicity, Amia, Bianca, Petra and Mercedes!

'THEY'RE UP THERE!' I shouted. 'ON THE LAUNCH PAD!' Everyone looked up. We could hardly see anything because the smoke was so thick over there, swirling round the high tower of the launch pad.

Desperate to hear the sound of the emergenbots' flying rescue craft, Mrs Fradley looked up into the blue sky and said, 'Oh, oh! Where are the emergency services?!'

'Maybe there's a lot of traffic on the flyway?' Mr Caldwell said nervously.

You could just make out the dark shapes of the stranded girls waving their arms for help, but the smoke was so thick it was impossible to tell who was who. We all watched wide-eyed as flames roared from the staff-room portal.

Mr Caldwell said quietly, 'Look! Now the old launch-pad steps are alight!' He ran forward to the launch-pad tower, coughing and waving his arms up at the girls on top. 'JUST STAY WHERE YOU ARE, GIRLS! THE EMERGENBOTS ARE ON THEIR WAY!' He walked back towards our class. 'Don't worry, children, the emergenbots will be here any second! The girls will be absolutely fine!' But I heard him sigh, 'I hope . . .'

I pushed out of my class line and ran towards the perimeter fence.

'LYLA HASTINGS! BACK IN LINE!' yelled Mr Caldwell, but he sounded far away.

Everything went quiet apart from the sound of my own breathing and booming heart. And I slipped through that loose fence and ran up Betty's garden, ducking the branches and skipping the old stones like a real cat. I knew what I had to do.

Betty wasn't there so I climbed up into the rocket, all trembly, and fired up the jets just like she'd shown me, whispering, 'Steady wrist, Lyla, steady!'

I took the rocket up! And once it had cleared the high bushes I steered it towards the launch pad.

Everything was in sharp focus. I flew dangerously low over the whole school standing in their class lines as I tried to stabilise my flight, and I saw all their faces looking up at me, all their mouths in little 'Oh! What the?!' shapes of surprise. And there was Mr Caldwell, shielding his eyes against the sunlight as I flew over him. I remember trying to find the button to put on the headlights with my right hand – to see in the smoke – as my left hand fumbled to set the right altitude to reach the top of the launch pad. I didn't know my hands could shake so much . . .

But I landed the rocket on the top of the smoke-covered launch pad! There was a terrible grinding noise and a shower of sparks as I came down at an angle, but I did it! Without crushing any of the girls. They were there, but all huddled together, coughing and wheezing and trying to shout, 'Help!'

'IN! GET IN!' I yelled. Out of the corner of one eye I saw the bright orange of a flame creeping over the top of the launch-pad steps.

'I'M SCARED!' wailed Petra, clinging onto Bianca.

'PETRA, LET GO OF ME!' said Bianca.

'We're going to die up here!' Petra wailed.

'GET IN!' I yelled again. 'NOW!'

Then Petra shoved Bianca away so hard she fell over and Petra scrambled up into the rocket. 'ONLY TWO SEATS?! SO GO! JUST GO!'

I gave her a look and said, 'We can wait for my friends!'

Petra turned to me. 'Listen, stupid, even you know you can't take off in a rocket this small if it's overloaded. GO! Take me down first! You can just come back for that lot after! GO!'

The smoke was now so dark and thick we could hardly see a thing. We could just hear Bianca and the others coughing and trying to climb up to get in.

Bianca's fingers hooked round the rim of the small hatch. 'Help them in, Petra! I'm firing up the jets!' I screamed.

But she didn't! She just tried to peel Bianca's fingers off the edge, and said, 'NO! If we all go in this junky old thing together we'll crash!'

I leaned across her and held my hand out so I could help Bianca in. Bianca fell into the rocket on top of Petra and was soon followed by the others, all wheezing and soot-stained.

They were all in a pile on the one small seat with Petra right at the bottom shouting, 'You're crushing my legs!'

Getting the rocket back up was a bit like our skycar with the faulty jet, only worse. The rocket took off at a dangerous tilt, the engines making a horrible grinding sound as they strained to lift us all. But they did!

We got just a few metres up and off the smoky launch pad and then I flew the rocket down to the playground, flying it low till we landed by the rows of children.

The girls untangled themselves from the front seat, and as we all scrambled down to the ground from the rocket the whole school did a massive cheer!

Bianca, who was standing right next to me, whispered, 'That was incredible! How did you learn to do that?'

'Wasn't allowed in the band so I had to do something in my lunch times,' I smiled.

Felicity, still crying, came and gave me a hug, a loud and embarrassing-hanging-onto-me-for-ages hug. 'You rescued us! Lyla! We've been so mean to you for weeks! But you rescued us! I feel soo-oo aaawful! I'm soo-o-oo sorryyyyyyy!'

Mrs Fradley ushered us into our class lines, then she looked up at the sky. We could all hear the long siren of the emergenbots flying towards us. 'Oh, thank goodness!' she cried. 'They're coming!'

And then it rained. Suddenly. It just poured down. Like rain I'd never seen. And from the corner of the playground came a soaking wet Louis, splashing through the puddles and shouting, 'OH, YES! THE ALL-TIME HERO! DON'T ALL THANK ME AT ONCE! Mr Caldwell, I did those playground weather settings again! HEAVY RAIN set for thirty minutes!'

'Good boy, Louis!' said Mr Caldwell, giving him a thumbs up.

The emergenbots arrived in their huge circular flying rescue craft. Blue lights flashed all around the edge. They did all the stuff you see them do on the news with the big hose things and the deoxygen vents. But really, thanks to me and Louis, there wasn't much for the emergenbots to do. The original fire, caused by Miss Fritz lying her overheated head onto a pile of soft cushions in the staff room, wasn't very big any more – and Louis' rain had contained it.

But it's always good to see the real emergenbots up close. The Year Ones were so excited they were all jumping up and down and trying to wave to them.

They make those emergenbots look really lovely – modern, all shiny, and they smell of lavender to calm people in a crisis. One of them came over to us girls and said, 'Must do a few health checks! Nothing will hurt.' It did all the scanning stuff and lasered away any cuts or bruises.

Felicity was still crying; she hadn't stopped since I got her down from the launch pad.

The emergenbot patted her head and said, 'Be calm. You are fine but your cyborg friend will need more care.'

Miss Fritz was winched up into the rescue craft on a stretcher under a white sheet thing. She had to be transferred to the Cyborg Restoration Unit in the Midlands Central Zone.

Louis' rain shower stopped and the sun came out again over the wet playground. Then we all turned to look towards the perimeter fence as Betty came crashing through the loose panel, shouting and looking very cross. 'All right! Which one of you thieving no-good brats stole my rocket? Ooooh, let me guess!' She walked straight up to me and placed her hands on her hips.

The little kids whispered, 'The BOGWITCH?' and stared at each other.

'I had to rescue my friends, Betty!' I stammered. 'I thought you might not mind!'

Betty looked at her rocket. 'Well, I DO mind! You've scratched it!' Then she looked around, taking in the scene. She looked at the burnt-out staff room and us with our sooty faces. 'You performed an actual rescue mission? You?! Well, kid, you're better than I thought!'

I smiled. 'I was very focused and I would have asked to borrow it if I'd had time. Sorry,' I said. 'And sorry for the scratch. I came in too fast.'

She seemed calmer. 'OK . . . that's OK! You did well. Flying in smoky conditions isn't easy.' She paused and patted her big hair. 'Well, I need it back right now as I've got an appointment at one of the finest vets in the Moon Colonies – only the best for my two kitten babies!'

And she climbed up into the rocket. We all watched as she took off. Up through the clouds, a vanishing dot, up to the Moon.

Petra wiped the mucky tear stains on her face with her hand and said crossly, 'I wish *I* was going home to the Moon. Earth is full of stupid people and it's dangerous! Who ever heard of a school being FLAMMABLE!'

And that was the last day she came into school! Mr and Mrs Lumen decided to send her to a very exclusive boarding school in Catena Yuri.

A fireproof one.

CHAPTER TWELVE

A week later there was a big assembly. Mrs Fradley explained how the new staff room was almost completed and this one would have a top-of-the-range coffee machine that took the orders from teachers by them just thinking about the perfect cappuccino ten minutes before a break. And all the teachers smiled and went, 'Ooh, lovely!'

Then she said it was time to put some special good deeds in our very special 'List of Golden Deeds'.

Mrs Fradley started calling people out. 'Samantha Yates, from Year One, for tidying up all the orange peel after break! Well done . . . !'

'Lyla Hastings and Louis MacAvoy, Year Six, for

rescue work and putting out a fire! Well done, guys! Good job . . . !'

'And finally, Evan Holmes, Year One, who's made great progress eating more vegetables at lunch time! Brilliant!'

We all stood in a line at the front. Everyone clapped us. Evan did a little bow and blew a kiss to the school. And I heard Gus shout out, 'Go, Evan! Vegetable-eating hero!'

Louis whispered, 'How is picking up orange peel or eating more peas the same as a fire rescue mission? Us two should be getting solid golden medals!'

Mrs Fradley said, 'Don't spoil it, Louis. No talking! You don't want to miss another break.'

We got down off the stage and then Mrs Fradley said, 'And now a really exciting part of today's assembly is welcoming back our fully restored Miss Fritz!'

Miss Fritz walked up onto the stage. But you could hardly tell it was Miss Fritz as her face had been re-done and she could walk quickly.

She spoke in a new fast voice, way more human-sounding. 'Hi, guys! Look, they've given me a total makeover! I'm solar-powered, so I won't need to recharge and I can now run up to fifty-five miles per hour! I have new thermal image sensors so I can see all of you through walls! I'll be able to see what you're all doing all the time and remember EVERYTHING because I have unlimited memory capacity!'

Louis shook his head and muttered to no one in particular, 'Uh oh, not good! She'll have me in every break till the end of the year!' Then he turned to me and said, 'Almost forgot!' and high-fived me.

'Why did you do that?'

'Check your palm!'
I looked down and there was a Palmprint with a little sparkly dinosaur.
'It's for my birthday party,' said Louis. 'You'll come, yeah?'
I nodded.

A MOON GIRL STOLE MY FRIEND

· ✳·☆·✳ *

The school made Betty Astral fix her fence so that no one could creep in again. The day before she had it mended, I took Bianca in the lunch break to say hello to her through the loose panel. We stood in the playground by the panel and yelled her name as loud as we could, 'BETT-Y! BETT-Y!'

Eventually we heard the leaves rustling as she came towards us through the bushes.

'Do you have to shout SO loud?' she said over the fence. She pushed the loose panel aside and waved us in, looked at us both and sighed. 'Just like stray cats – you're nice to one and then before you know it they bring a friend!'

'Yes, this is my friend, Bianca!' I said.

'Oh?' Betty said. 'I thought you said you didn't have any friends?'

'I didn't!' I said. 'Well, I did . . . then I didn't, and . . . now I do!'

'I was a bit mean,' said Bianca, looking sideways.

'But she apologised!' I said. 'Lots.'

'But I was being really, really mean,' said Bianca. 'For ages.'

'But she changed and like you said, nothing stays the same! And it didn't!' I smiled.

'Well, I'm glad you two made it up because I've had Lyla moping about here for days all lonesome and getting in my way!' said Betty, smiling. 'And now you two have made it up, Lyla won't need to come bothering me.'

I said, 'Once they fix the fence I can't see you ever again anyway.'

'Too right!' said Betty.

'Really? You don't want me to visit you ever again?' I said. 'I like you. I like your cats.'

'Well,' said Betty, leaning on the fence, 'it might be nice if somebody invited me round to *their* garden for a change.'

'I'll ask my mum!' I said. 'If you come, will you come in the rocket? Gus would love to see that! Will you bring the real kittens?'

'I'll think about it,' she said, and began walking back up the overgrown garden.

'She's not very friendly,' whispered Bianca.

'She is,' I said. 'She just pretends not to be.'

· ✳·⭐.✳ *

Bianca and I had a sleepover at hers that Friday night and she had some of the Insta-Locks left and she let me have it! Now I have swishy hair, no sprouty bit! And I'm keeping it like this! Even though Gus says, 'It looks very, very, very bad and ugly and girly.'

And on Saturday morning, me and Bianca pedalled our flykes to the Trading Hub to get some hair accessories for my new long hair.

On Saturday afternoon I went to Louis' birthday party. I was the only girl there. I had to talk about rockets a lot. James Defries kept saying stuff like, 'Yeah, but on the newer intergalactics they don't have any manual control,' like *he* could fly anything.

Louis threw a jellyfish crispy at his head and said, 'Like you know, James! You only ever take your flyke up two metres!'

Gus was really jealous because Louis' mum had got Mr Dinosaur to come. Mr Dinosaur made a half-size Diplodocus. We got to feed it. When I told Gus it also got loose in their kitchen and ate most of the cake and did a dinosaur poo he said, 'Now that's a *good* party!'

And then on the Sunday Bianca came to my house and we made loads of little cupcakes for Betty, and then we made sure it all looked nice for her visit and Mum moved our skycar a bit on the launch pad so Betty would have room to land her rocket when she arrived.

She arrived at three in the afternoon. Even Dad was excited because, 'It's not every day you get to meet a space legend!'

I think Betty had tried to smarten herself up with some bright orange lipstick and lots of perfume. When she saw our modern flat roof with its own launch pad she said, 'Aren't we all a bit swanky?!' Then she gave Dad a bunch of blue bananas as a gift. 'The blue ones taste so much better!'

She said she hadn't actually visited anyone for about thirty years, so Gus and Bianca and I gave her a tour of the house. She was very impressed with my room. We introduced her kittens to Sparks but the real kittens tried to chew Sparks' ears so we put Sparks to bed, and Gus tried to get the real kittens to sleep on his head except he didn't have enough hair. And one did a wee on his ear. So he stopped trying.

Betty ate loads of our cakes and said, considering we were people and not cats, we weren't too bad. Then she left, climbing back into her rocket.

Dad said, 'Do come again!'

'Thank you! I'll think about it!' she shouted as she fired up the jets and was gone.

· ✳·⭐·✳ ·

Next time Betty went to the Moon she bought Bianca and me two of those crystal bikinis. Just like Petra had. She said it was just a little thank you for, 'Giving me a real jolly time last Sunday!'

And next Saturday Bianca and I are going to flyke together to the Havendome, and Bianca's granny says we can wear the crystal bathing suits in her colour-change pool! Plus we have this great new game. We call it 'Ladies of Mars'. In the game I'm called Belinda Alvor and Bianca is called Laura Pavonis.

Mostly we put on lipstick and talk about our new kitchens. In stupid voices. It's hilarious.

To us.